Wolf Queen

THE CLÁIDI JOURNALS ✳ BOOK III

Wolf Queen

Tanith Lee

DUTTON CHILDREN'S BOOKS ✳ NEW YORK

To Beverley Birth—
who has been a best friend to these books

Copyright © 2001 by Tanith Lee

CIP Data is available.

Published in the United States 2002 by Dutton Children's Books,
a division of Penguin Young Readers Group
345 Hudson Street, New York, New York 10014
www.penguin.com

Originally published in Great Britain 2001
by Hodder Children's Books, London

Designed by Ellen M. Lucaire
Printed in USA • First American Edition
5 7 9 10 8 6
ISBN 0-525-46895-1

UP IN THE AIR.
Traditional

CONTENTS

Wolf Queen

THIS NEW BOOK

The world is so far below, down there.

Sometimes I feel this ship will never land there again.

It's the first time we've *crossed* land for nine days. Before that it was just water—the ocean, day after day and every night. And this is the first entry I've made in this new book, which is to be my new diary-journal-whatever.

There's a sunset starting now. The sky is a deep *sky*-blue, with biscuity-gold high clouds above, quite still. But a wind from the land has blown one different, low, large red cloud toward us, and now the cloud has wrapped right around the ship. We've been in the cloud for several minutes, since we sail-fly very slowly. It's like being in a rose-red fog.

✦ ✦ ✦

When I was writing on the last page of the *last* book, I said I'd describe my journey in this Star—this sky-ship.

Only, as I say, until now there wasn't much to see. Only the water. Too high to make out anything definite, except, sometimes, in sunshine, altered colors in the sea like drifting dyes.

Before the sea, there was just the top of the jungle.

This coast, when we reached it, looked bare and bleak at first. Then there were forests—Yinyay says that's what they are.

As the light goes, the forests seem to be separating.

A broad river flashed below in the last twilight gleam. And—how odd—I saw the small shadow of the Star, in which I am, pass over the river's surface.

The main thing is, I have to find Argul. Which means finding the Hulta.

And then, once I've told him properly what happened, well I—we—have to think of some way to be safe. Because if the Wolf Tower sent kidnappers after me once, why not a second time? Or will they just think now I'm too much trouble, not worth the effort, and leave me alone?

Somehow, leaving the Rise, I never thought about this possibly ongoing threat from the Wolf Tower.

But I was very muddled, particularly about Venn.

I'm still muddled about Venn.

He's Argul's half-brother. I keep reminding myself of that. That's why they look so alike, and that was why I sort of fell for Venn. Yes, I did fall for him. (Can say that now he's miles away.)

But there was absolutely nothing between us, beyond the polite good-bye kiss he gave me.

I kept wondering today if we would miss signs of the Hulta, because we're up so high. But when I spoke to Yinyay, she said the machines on the Star will spot the Hulta instantly.

"How?" I asked.

"You have told me a great deal about them," said Yinyay. "This information is fed into the ship, which, even now, is alert to seek and recognize them."

"Even from up here?"

"Of course."

The Star-ship is incredible and can do so much—rising and landing, lighting itself at night, making food, judging a thousand and one things perfectly.

And Yinyay herself, being mechanical, is sort of part of the ship—*linked* to the ship, the way Venn's mother, Ustareth, made her to be. Though Yinyay looks like a silvery doll snake (quite a large one, standing on her tail taller than me) with a sweet face and voice, and though she does nice, helpful, funny things, like handing you a cup of tea held in her extended hair—Yinyay is massively powerful, too. *Reliable.* So I believed her. If the Hulta are down there, the Star will "recognize" them.

Later she even said something about the Star's having worked out the most likely places for the Hulta to be, right now, taking into consideration what had happened, how long I'd been gone, and their ways of traveling generally. Which means we stand an even better chance of tracking them down.

So, nothing to worry about at all.

✦ ✦ ✦

Dinner just came, as always, out of a slot in the silver-pearly wall.

It's dark now, that red cloud left far behind.

Through the cleared curved window-walls at the "front" of the Star, I can watch all night, if I want, while sitting on a comfortable padded bench.

Maybe I'll see the tiny lights of settlements, towns, or villages down on the ground. Maybe I'll see—the lights of the Hulta camp, the little fires and lamps, and the big central fire where they hold their councils, and maybe even (*unseen by me at this distance*) Argul will actually be standing there, their leader, tall and straight and bright with gold, his long black hair gleaming.

I have found Argul! We are together again! Perhaps the very next thing I write here will be that. Why oh why don't I think it will be?

HULTA WELCOME

It was the Star, of course, that found them. I wasn't even watching at the time, but in the bathroom, soaking determinedly in a warm, scented bath. (Trying to calm down.)

I shot out when Yinyay told me, didn't wait for the warm air-jets to dry me properly, flung on clothes and ran into the main area with my hair wringing wet.

"Where? Where???"

This was three and a half days after my first entry in this book. It was afternoon, and below lay a sunny flatness, a plain, with occasional greenish puffs that must be woods, or the last of the forest.

"Wherewherewhere—"

"There."

I couldn't see anything that made any sense. (It had also been mostly impossible for me to see anything identifiable, by night or day, even lights, unless there were hundreds of them together.) However, Yinyay now guided me, and then I saw a far-off splodge, like more woods only browner.

"Is that—?"

"That is."

The Star began to descend, a little slantingly, toward the splodge.

The splodge in turn began to excite and upset me so much I was shaking, and water drops spun off my washed hair all over the room, so soon it looked as if rain had fallen.

Yinyay extended her own tendrilly hair, which can do lots of useful things, and soft drying waves of heat played over mine. But I couldn't stay still.

I ran about, from curved window to window. And then I ran away, thinking I ought to fetch something—what?—and then back again.

All this while, the Star flew on and down nearer to—

The Hulta.

I could see licks of color in the brownness now, suggestions of movement—the roll of wheels and wagons, trot and pull of horses, running of dogs and children—

Oh God. At last. But—I wasn't ready—

"How long do I have?" I cried. "I mean, before we get close—land—"

"Some twenty and one-quarter minutes," said Yinyay, precisely.

"Oh—no—that's not long enough—I must—I have to—"

What did I "have to"? Nothing. I had packed my bag; even this book (and the last book) were in there, and about nine million ink pencils of various kinds. And anyway, nothing had been said about the Star's rushing away the moment I stepped out. Yinyay had already told me the Star would simply land and wait, until I came back and told it what I wanted next.

What would the Hulta think, when they saw the Star, a great spiky starry thing, bowling along the sky, by day, violently sparkling from the sun, a planet presumably come unfixed from outer space?

Would the kids be scared? The well-trained, well-loved dogs start howling? Would Argul ride between his people and the Star, strong and wonderful and *good*, to protect them, with Blurn, his second-in-command, black and handsome, wild, brave, and over-the-top, at his side?

"Can't we go any *faster?*" I now blathered.

"It's best," said Yinyay, gently, "not to descend too quickly. The magnets are most efficient when at leisure."

The magnets are how the Star rises and descends. Have never understood this—and right then everything Yinyay said sounded ridiculous.

But I just rushed away again and then rushed back again.

And then I just kneeled on a bench, craning over the steely desk that has controls in it, and peered down and down at the splodge getting bigger, and becoming the Hulta.

Suddenly, I could see it had *become* the Hulta. There they were. Tiny as fleas, but really there.

Then I even made out some of the wagons I knew, from various marks. Like Badger's wagon, which had a long patched tear in the leather top, where a bough once fell in a storm, and one of the women's wagons, too, which I'd once shared, and which was painted across with stripes.

Obviously by now the Star had been seen in turn.

Face upon face, small as grains of rice, staring up. Kids I could just see, pointing. Riders riding in to form a kind of ring around children and animals. An abrupt spark here, there, *there*—which were sun-catching knives being drawn, and bells and disks shaken on bridles as horses reared.

Yes, I'd been stupid.

"Yinyay, can we stop, please, I mean stop the Star."

Yinyay did something with her hair on the desks. We stopped.

"I don't want to go any closer like this. It's scaring people and causing too much bother. In fact—Yinyay, sorry, but can we back right off?"

We were lifting, ascending, retreating.

The crowds of rice-grain faces were folding back into—a splodge.

"Let's come down—say, over there? Is that all right? Then I can go across to them on foot. Look, it's downhill. It'll only take me half an hour. And . . . I could do with a walk."

I tried to sound organized and efficient. I was cursing myself for my selfish idiocy, putting myself first, not thinking. Frightening my friends with this big, terrifying sky-object.

In the confusion, I hadn't had a chance to find Argul, there among all those toy wagons and toy humans. If I had, would he, too, have looked only like that? Like a tiny, moving toy?

+ + +

We landed, smooth as silk. Inside ten minutes I was walking downhill, through some rather odd trees with no leaves, but covered in something like green foam—

Then I met the Hulta head-on.

That is, I met twenty Hulta, seventeen men and three women, on horseback and with drawn weapons. The front four men had rifles, pointing ready at me. And the first of these men was Blurn.

"*Clll—aidii*—oh yarollakkus," said Blurn, on a long, astonished, sighing-boom.

I thought, I've never heard *that* before, yarollakkus. Probably rude. I didn't ask.

"Hi, Blurn," I said shyly. Feeling a total fool. Back five seconds, and already I'd caused all this fuss.

Over their shoulders I could see the Hulta wagons downslope, in a defensive huddle.

"What in—what are you *doing* here?" asked Blurn.

"Blurn, I'm sorry, it was stupid to arrive like that. I was rattled and didn't think. *Sorry.*"

He gaped at me and I at him.

"What do you mean what am I *doing* here?"

"I mean what the hell are you doing here."

Something reached me then, at last.

Something I had never felt from, or among, the Hulta, not even at the very start, although, at the very start, I hadn't known I hadn't. What I mean is, I had thought, when I first met the Hulta, they were murderer-bandits and insane. (None of which was true.) But I'd assumed they would therefore be dangerous. Half-imagined they were, until I learned otherwise.

Now—they *were* dangerous.

I looked at them, and all at once I saw how it wasn't any more simply that they'd been unnerved, expecting to have to fight and guard their people from a skyborne alien threat. It wasn't even astonishment at my abrupt return, or annoyance at my thoughtlessness.

No. It was—

It was dangerous, unliking, *angry, hating* hostility.

"Blurn . . . ," I said, uncertainly.

"All right. All right, Claidi. Hey," said Blurn, turning back to the others, "how about giving her and me a bit of room?"

And then one of the men spoke.

Most of the men there I didn't know that well—I'd looked in vain for Ro or Mehmed. But this was Badger, whose wagon I had seen. Badger, who I did know quite well.

"Don't trust the rotten little okkess," said Badger, giving me a *look*—what a *look*—and then turning in his saddle and spitting on the ground.

I went cold as ice. It wasn't from my wet hair.

And, well, I knew what *okkess* meant. Not many women would want a friend to call them that.

I just stood there.

Blurn said, "I said, I'll deal with it. Claidi? Walk over there with me, will you?"

They sat their horses and watched as Blurn dismounted, and he and I walked aside along the slope. Some of them kept their rifles pointed at the place where the Star had landed. One of the women stared at me, and when I looked back, I saw it was Ashti, Blurn's partner, who had always been so nice to me.

Who had gone to the pool with me that morning of my wedding day, the day when I was captured and carried off—and Ashti's face was like a dark stone mask.

Her face was worse than the name Badger had called me.

I felt sick. But I didn't know why I should.

So I halted and turned and caught hold of Blurn's arm. And he picked my hand off with dreadful quiet strength.

He still wore his hair in all those scores of glorious braids. His eyes were like polished bullets.

"Blurn, I don't know why you're acting like this." He just looked at me. "Why is everyone—like this? Is it because of the Star—the ship—I said I was sorry—"

"*That* thing," he said, as if I'd mentioned some old wreck of a wagon I'd arrived in.

I hesitated, swallowed. I said, "All right. Just take me to see Argul."

Then Blurn flung back his head and he laughed. He laughed like crazy, and the sky reeled.

"Argul is not, at present, here."

"Then where?"

Something seemed after all to break through his eyes. He said, "Claidi, are you really so tronking daft that you don't know what you did to him?"

"What?—what *I* did—"

"Left him. Like that. You couldn't even tell him to his face, could you, that you were through? Did you think he'd attack you? He wouldn't have gone near you. You're stupid all right. Real stupid, Claidi."

I stopped looking at Blurn because that wasn't helping.

Looking at anything was a problem. The trees were all covered with this bubbling frothy stuff. And the Hulta were bursting with hatred. I shut my eyes and said, "Look, Blurn, I didn't *want* to leave Argul. Some air balloons came over and some very big men in uniform, from the Wolf Tower City, grabbed me and dragged me off. I did my best, but there was no one who could help. Didn't Ashti tell you? She was *there*."

"Yeah. All the women told us. The balloons and how you all ran. Then they thought you'd got left behind."

"I *had* been. In a net. Then I was tied up in the balloon and up in the sky. I'll tell you the rest later."

"No, thanks. We know the rest. A friend, you see, of your *best pal* from the Tower—he told us."

I tried to hold on. "I don't have pals from the Tower. Who was it?"

"Look, girl," said Blurn, "in a minute they're going to come over and skin you. Get in your flashy star-thing and go away."

I'm hardly brilliant, but even I could see something had seemed to happen that hadn't. But I was shocked—so shocked even the panic wasn't boiling up in me yet. I sounded nearly calm as I said, "At least tell me where Argul is."

"Could be anywhere. After you dumped him, he left the Hulta in my charge and went off by himself. That was months ago, Claidi. None of us have seen him since then."

Calm went. "But didn't you try to stop him?" I screamed.

"You couldn't stop Argul, when he'd really decided. Besides, Hulta law says that if a leader doesn't want to lead anymore, he gives it up. So I'm leader now, which I never wanted. He was my friend."

Away along the slope Ashti called suddenly in a clear stone voice, "Do you want *me* to see to her, Blurn?"

He turned and shook his head at her. To me he said, "I tell you, Claidi, I was surprised at you. Going off with that okk Nemian again, after the way he was last time."

I nearly jumped out of my body into one of the weird trees. I spluttered. I cried, "*Nemian*—I wouldn't touch Nemian with a six-man-height-length flagpole for goodness sake—Is *this* what you think? I ran off and left Argul on our wedding day because I *wanted* to? Wanted to be with *Nemian* in the *Wolf Tower*? Are you *mad*?"

"Are *you*?" he said.

I shivered.

"No."

"I think you must be. Look, I *know*, so there's no point you lying. You see, this dupp from the Tower turned up soon after you went. He swanned in with his little escort and told us the lot. He said you were done with us. And if we didn't believe him, look in your diary-book, which you'd carelessly left in the rush to get back to Nem. And yes, I've read your book. You'd written it out plain enough. On and on about how you really wanted Nemian, couldn't stop thinking of him, and Argul was all right, you'd put up with him. Second best. And then you just couldn't help it, you sent this loveletter to Nemian—"

"I NEVER sent any—"

"And they got you word he'd send someone along. And how you wanted to go to that pool because you knew the balloon could get down to you there easily, none of us around to get in the way. Pity you left the diary, eh? Or we'd never have completely believed a story like that."

"I didn't leave my diary behind. It went with me. So what *diary* are you talking about?"

"The book you were always scribbling in."

"What you found wasn't that—wasn't *mine*. I can *show* you my diary. They must somehow have made one like it. Dropped it in the right place to be found."

"It was in your writing. Even I knew it. And Argul certainly did."

Argul—I had to do something—but I was shaking so hard suddenly that all that came out was stammering.

I was trying to tell him that the Towers, the Rise, could do incredible things—make copies probably of handwriting, diaries that would seem to be the original diary. And it sounded lame. Absurd. I knew he didn't believe me.

Blurn folded his arms. It was like gazing at a bolted door. He said, "Where's the ring Argul gave you?"

I stood there and said nothing. I knew I couldn't explain to him why I had taken the ring off. He wouldn't believe that either. Anything I said, he wouldn't believe, even if I said the sky was blue.

I felt as I sometimes had when I was quite little, in the House. Utterly hopelessly powerless. At the mercy of rules I didn't understand and people who didn't ever want to bother to understand me. It was like that. And worse, because Blurn had been my friend, and Argul's friend, and Blurn hated me. And I couldn't find any more words.

"I've had enough of you, girl," he said then. "If that star-ship junk isn't going to bother us, get back in it and clear off."

He turned. He strode along the slope, making as he went a sweeping signal to the others.

I watched them go, without a single backward glance at me. And there I was alone, under those disgusting frothy trees.

MIDNIGHT DAGGER

Someone else has read my diary. Like Venn did. Funny really—since this time, it *wasn't* MY diary at all.

I have been trying and trying for hours, crouched here in the closed-off area of the ship, to put it all together.

The Wolf Tower grabbed me so they could punish me, then they were double-crossed by someone else, who captured me instead. Either way, it was against my will. I was shipped (by a real sea-ship) to the Rise, and stuck there, till Venn helped me reach this Star and come back here.

Blurn and the Hulta, though—and that means Ashti, Teil, Toy—all of them—think this: I left willingly to go by balloon back to Nemian, that utter creep, and live in his City with him.

And someone—the Wolf Tower—or that other unknown lot who took me away from the Wolf Tower's men and sent me to the Rise—left a diary so like mine it convinced even Argul. Argul has never read my diary. But he often saw it. Saw me writing in it. Knows my writing. And this *fake* diary is written in my writing—or so near, they didn't see any difference.

And the fake diary says I loved Nemian. Wrote to Nemian and told him so. And he arranged for me to be with him.

Next thing, I appear again, in the Star, which I suppose the Hulta think is also from the City.

And Argul—

Argul thinks I am with Nemian, whom I love.

Oh no.

They all hate me. And—it's all because of a lie.

This is like the Rise, when Venn believed their lies about me—the lies of the Tower, or someone who signed themselves "We."

Also, it's much worse. Because these people were my friends. They were the first and only family I ever had.

Am I guilty in some peculiar way? Is it . . . because I fell—not for Nemian—but for Venn?

No. *Rubbish.*

I didn't fall for him *that* hard.

Why does the Wolf Tower, or whoever it is, *want* everyone to think I've done these idiotic and horrible things? Just to pay me back?

Where is Argul?

✦ ✦ ✦

I'd actually fallen asleep, curled up on the bed-couch by the wall. Was having a nasty dream about something, I forget what, but it left a bad feeling all through me.

". . . What?"

"Someone is here, Claidi."

Yinyay's sweet face floated over me on her mechanical serpent-like body, in the Star's dimmed lamps. Was it midnight? Felt like it.

"Who? Aren't they—?"

"Armed," remarked Yinyay mildly. As if it didn't mean anything much. "She was requested to lay down her weapon and has done so. She will do you no harm. She's been told, the ship protects you."

Of course upset, but puzzled, I got up and wandered out into the main chamber. No one there.

The opening stood wide in the ship's side. I looked through and down the ramp, and out at the night plain.

"*Dagger.*"

"'Lo, Claidi," said Dagger.

She stood there, grimly planted and gazing up at me.

She was just eight when I went—was taken—away. Halfway toward nine now, I supposed. But she was always like someone much older. Older than me, definitely.

"Er, Dagger. Er, what . . . ?"

"I'm not coming into that machine," said Dagger. "Will you come out? I won't hurt you. I gave that snake-thing my Hulta word."

"Oh—yes."

Yinyay was there at once. She slipped a coat around my shoulders. She can be (occasionally, oddly) motherly. (But then,

I've always thought Ustareth designed Yinyay to care for Venn, when he was quite young, in case he had found the Star then, gone traveling in it.)

"Thanks. . . ."

On the ground. The night was chilly; I was glad of the coat. Dagger herself wore a jacket and long waistcoat and a cloak. "What *is* that thing in there?" she asked. "*Is* it a *snake?*"

"No—a sort of mechanical doll—like at Peshamba."

"Doesn't look like that."

"No."

Dagger said, "Don't you want to know why I came up here? No one else would. And if they knew *I* had, they'd say I was a right dope."

Surprised, I realized Dagger wasn't swearing in her usual vivid manner.

She had been with me, like Ashti, Toy, and Teil, by the pool, on my wedding day. My *un*-wedding day.

"Then why did you?" I asked humbly.

"I want to ask you, Claidi, if it's true."

"Which bit?"

She scowled but said, "Did you dump Argul and run off to that twit Nemian?"

"What do you *think*, Dagger?"

"Well, it looks as if you did."

"Yes, doesn't it. Well I *didn't*." Something in me flared up all at once, and I began to rant on and on, all the things I might have shouted at Blurn. How I would *never* have left, and if I had, I'd have done it differently—didn't any of them remember me at *all?* Did they really think I was that foul?

I said I loved Argul and only wanted Argul. I told the story of what had happened, the abduction, balloon, ship, the jungles, in rather more detail than I'd been able to offer Blurn. I didn't say much about Venn. Just that I hadn't at first been able to escape from the Rise, and that as soon as I could, I'd come back.

Dagger stood there, frowning. I could make this out by the faint Star-light (from the ship) and the broader starlight of the sky.

"You mean you were just stuck there, in this palace place, and all that time, and you didn't try to get away or *do* anything?"

"It was impossible, Dagger. Really it was. I couldn't see where to go—I didn't know what to do."

"Doesn't sound like you," she said, damningly.

"Well it *was* me. I'm telling you. And the other stuff about running off to Nemian *wasn't* me. Wasn't. Isn't."

"Yes," said Dagger. She stared into the night.

"Look, Dagger, if you don't believe me, then just go away."

"I believe you."

"Because this is bad enough without—yes?"

"I believe you. Sounds all wrong and mad, but then you running off like that 'cos you *wanted* to was madder and wronger."

I felt sick now with relief. Couldn't speak.

Away through the distances of the night, sliced over and over by the thin stems of the froth trees, veiled by their almost transparent foliage, I could make out the glow of the great Hulta campfire, maybe a half-mile off.

"Is there any chance anyone else might believe you?" Dagger asked my yearning unspoken question. "No chance, Claidi.

They can't see it somehow. Don't know why not. Argul going away like he did probably put them off you."

"Why did he, Dagger? Why couldn't *he* see, if *you* can—"

"Oh," she said. She shrugged.

She meant, I think, he's grown-up and so not quite so clever as he was. And for the first time I guessed Dagger's adult wisdom comes from her being a *kid*.

That's why she's made allowances for me, too. My age.

I'm grateful.

We walked off a little way and sat down on a smoothish stone in the dark.

"Here," said Dagger.

I thought she was going to stab me after all. Then I saw it was her other dagger she'd taken out, the one she'd given me as a wedding gift. It had been really shined up, and it still was.

"Wanted you to have that," she said. "I gave it to you before, so it's still yours."

"Oh, Dagger—thanks!"

"I'd have brought your horse, your Sirree. But someone would have seen and stopped me. Anyhow, I don't think Sirree'd want to go in that Star contraption."

"No."

I held the dagger Dagger had given me. Weapons don't often appeal to me. But this one—was like a slice of old friendship, high-polished. I felt I'd never let it go.

"Listen, Claidi-baa," said Dagger. "If you ever *need* a horse—try the towns northeast. You get good horses there. Some of the Hulta ones come from there, when we need new stock."

"Uh—thanks, Dagger."

"And," she said casually, kicking her legs on the side of the stone, "you might just find him, there."

"Do you mean Argul?"

"Yep. Could be. Hulta trade there a bit. We're going west right now. But he might have gone that way. East, north. There's a place. It's called Panther's Halt." I waited, speechless. "Y'see, his mum had a house there."

"Zeera," I breathed.

Zeera, Argul's mother, who had once been Ustareth, the mother of Venn.

They hate the Tower City. They don't know that *she* originally came from there. That lovely Zeera, who they liked such a lot, was a woman born in the Wolf Tower.

And now really wasn't the time to tell Dagger.

"So you think Argul might have gone northeast to—Panther's Halt. Was he—" I faltered. I said, in a whisper, "*How* was he?"

"Sore," she said. "What do you think?"

"But to stop being leader—"

"Yes," she said. "That was bad. 'Specially since you say everything was a put-up job."

"Oh, Dagger, thank God you believe me."

"Well, you're not always so bright, but you're not a hundred percent *crazy*."

I hugged her. She let me a moment. Then pulled away. She picked up her own knife from where she had left it on the ground. "Well, I guess it's so long for now."

We shook hands.

As I walked back to the Star, I heard a faint music from the

Hulta camp. A dance, drums and pipes and clapping. Maybe to show the Star they weren't afraid of it, were carefree, being so tough and well able to fight. Or to show me once and forever that now I was an outsider of the Hulta Family.

I knew, didn't I, that something was wrong, all the time I was getting here. I don't know how I knew.

But now I shall find Argul. I shall convince Argul. One day, I'll bring him back to them and make them see the truth.

Do you believe me? I mean it. Stay with me, please, my unknown friend that I talk to, that perhaps one day will read these, my *real* diaries, and trust me not to be lying. Stay with me.

I ran up the ramp of the Star.

"Yinyay! Can we find a town called Panther's Halt?"

DOWN TO EARTH

Five days now, gliding *so slowly* through the sky, heading northeast.

Lots of water below, lakes, I think, and rivers, then marshland, very green. Then—another of those awful deserts. From up here, like a cement floor littered with grey rubble, but the larger mounds must be hills, mountains perhaps.

Once, we were a bit lower and herds of things were running, disturbed maybe by the Star. But I couldn't make out what they were.

The sun came up to the right and sank on the left. Now it rises more in front of us as the Star veers east.

✦ ✦ ✦

No doubt about this ship being able to locate Panther's Halt. It can find almost anywhere, virtually anything.

I did ask if it could simply trace—Argul. Apparently not, unless he wore a Tag the ship was set to recognize. (Like the Tag the Wolf Tower had someone put in my first diary, unknown to me, by which they traced me to the pool and were able to nab me.)

So I'm glad the Star can't find him without some gadget or by skillful guesswork. It means some things can be concealed from the frightening frightful science-magic of the Towers, and people like Ironel Novendot, and Ustareth-Zeera.

(All those years with the Hulta, when U-Zeeera used her abilities only to help them. And lied, or hid the astonishing other things she could do—make jungles, breed monsters, make a doll that was her own double—was she really by then tired of her science, as Venn said he thought she was?)

A large flock of big, black, croaking birds flew by earlier. They're ravens. I've seen birds like these in Peshamba, and here and there.

Yinyay says these ones come from the north.

There was a Raven Tower once, in the City, but apparently, in the historic wars between the Towers (Wolf Tower, Boar Tower, Tiger Tower), the Raven Tower was destroyed.

Might as well stop writing.

Nothing much to say.

All I can think of, all I want to write is—What am I going to say to him when we meet? How can I prove to him I didn't do what he thinks? Is he going to believe me? Or—is he going to act the same as Blurn?

* * *

It was late morning when it happened. I was sitting in the main area, looking at some more pictures of people from the Towers and aristocratic Houses, etc., having nothing better to do. This time the pictures showed in a little panel in one of the metal desks.

Suddenly I lost the picture, which had been of a tall man, with what looked like a rhinoceros on a leash. Then the lights bloomed all over the desk, and the other desks; very decorative it was.

"Oh, look, Yinyay."

I don't think I was all that startled. I mean, the whole of the Star is a mystery to me. Should have realized anything like this could only mean trouble.

Yinyay swayed from desk to desk. Then she activated her hatch and abruptly slid down through the floor to the even-stranger areas in the lower part of the ship, where no one else is allowed.

Presently she came up again and went into one of the cupboards in the second room.

By then, all the viewing window-walls had cleared. We'd decided to blank them out earlier, because the east-rising sun was so bright. Now, staring out, I saw that we were much lower. Lower than we'd been at any time, except when we landed for the Hulta.

And then I saw we *were* landing.

Which was peculiar, because this didn't seem to be the most absolutely best place for it.

We were over another forest of some kind, thick and tangled. And now the upper branches were brushing against the ship. And now they were *thrashing* the window-walls, and showers of leaves and pine-needles were spraying up. Hundreds of birds erupted all around us!

I yelled and threw myself flat. And the next thing was a series of crucial shudders and thumps, a sound like a piece of the Star being *ripped* right *off*—a seething in of shadow and darkness—and then a horrible bumping crunch of impact.

I was sliding, and then I hit something and stopped. What I'd hit was Yinyay.

"Are you all right, Yinyay?"

"I am of course quite fine. You are fine too, except for a bruise on your left elbow and one on your right elbow—"

"Ow. Yes, I know about the elbow bruises—"

"And left knee."

"Wooa*ouch*."

"That is the worst one."

"Yes, Yinyay, thanks, I *know*."

She slithered silkily over me and went to inspect the desks and things.

"The ship has lost power. The magnets have failed. This never occurred before," said Yinyay, sounding sad.

I stood up. "How long," all jollily confident, "will it take to put right?" I asked.

Yinyay came out of a cupboard and offered me some cream for the bruises. I rubbed it in, still confident. She was so faultlessly clever, she had even been able to work out where I'd been bruised before *I* did.

But Yinyay said, "Princess Ustareth's ship never fails. I have therefore no knowledge of what must be done to repair it."

"But—but you—but—"

"To alter things, of course," went on Yinyay, calmly, nearly wistfully, "to adapt. But a failure is never possible. I have no thought process to remedy such an event."

Great.

We sat there. Well, I sat there on the floor, and Yinyay coiled around a bench, and we gazed at each other, I and this amazing mechanized being. Both of us now entirely (as Ro would have said) up a cuckoo tree.

A while later, some lunch zoomed out of the slot in the wall.

So that still worked.

I nibbled the nut-cheese bread toast and drank the iced tea. I had to admit, though I hadn't the heart to say it, the tea was a little warm and the toast rather cold. So, even here the Star wasn't working quite as it had. No doubt the food supplies would also soon break down.

Without saying anything to Yinyay, I went to the bathroom and ran some water. It seemed all right. But then a small lizard splashed out of the tap.

"Oh."

Yinyay arrived around me, gathered the lizard gently in her hair, and deposited it outside the ship.

With the doorway open, I looked into the forest.

Shafts of noon light pierced through the trees. They were high bluish pines and wide coppery beeches, and straddled moss banks and dells. A pleasant scene. It was quiet now but for birds, singing on and on to get over the shock of a Star (us) crashing among them.

Was it worth asking Yinyay *why* the Star's powers had failed? Probably not.

"Is there anything that can be done?" I now unconfidently asked.

"No," said Yinyay.

I noticed then the final and most worrying—I mean *terrifying* thing—Yinyay seemed to be—well she *was*—sort of shrinking.

It had happened very suddenly. But so had the crash.

"Yinyay—you, um—what are you doing?"

"I regret, Claidi, I am automatically being shut down."

"Which means?"

"My power has always been connected to the ship's power. For now, I shall rest in the storage section, where I shall learn what may be done. This may take years, or longer. And since the storage section is a very small section—" her voice too was getting littler and littler—"I too must become very small. It will be interesting," she added, obviously cheered by the notion, "to learn so much of the ship. While in this tinier form, I shall have the ability to move through the inside of the walls—"

"Yinyay, you said years—"

"Almost certainly much longer."

"Can't you—"

"I am so sorry, Claidi. Perhaps there are other possibilities. . . . But it will have to be good-bye for now. It has been"— a teeny little squeak: "So nice knowing you."

She was little as a worm, smaller even than the lizard that, twenty minutes ago, she had competently raised and deposited outside.

Then a weeny slot opened in the floor. And with a bye-bye flick of her itty tail—she was gone.

Oh hell.

After about an hour, I went and changed my clothes. In the Star, Yinyay had seen to it I had dresses to wear, but also there were still the clothes I'd worn going through the jungle with Venn, a tunic and trousers and high boots. I added the coat.

Through the belt I put the dagger Dagger had given back to me.

I also packed my bag with my most important stuff, and a sandwich, and a bottle of the tea—I didn't trust the tap water anymore, and I didn't (ridiculously) know how to get more food before the dinner hour.

I tied my hair back.

Outside, the forest looked suspiciously adorable.

Cute little brownish squirrels were playing through the trees, and the birds sang and sang. But I thought: Claidi, you know this doesn't mean much. Around the next artistic bush may lurk some hulking THING. This is what my utterly silly life has taught me so far.

I've never before *traveled* alone.

Now I have to.

Hope Yinyay is all right.

I might even have stayed until tomorrow. It was not knowing how to close the door-opening for the night that decided me.

(In a way I feel disloyal to Yinyay, too. But what else can I do?)

At least I have a direction to take. East now, that's the way

I have to go. (I think.) The afternoon is young, the sun smiles through the forest, which, compared to a jungle, is easy.

Come on then. Put this new book into bag with first book. Sling bag over shoulder and secure buckle. Down ramp and into forest and off we go. Not once looking back.

FOREST WITH PANTHER

As I'd assumed, the walking part was easy. The hardest pieces of terrain were where I had to pick over large, old tree roots, step through a shallow stream or two, and climb a small hill.

The wildlife was nice, and also nonbig. Squirrels: a couple of little red catlike things with striped tails, playing up a beech tree; birds; a beast with bristles, snuffling about in some ancient leaves—I think that was a small porcupine. Mice.

I actually enjoyed walking. Sitting in the Star day after day had made me a bit rusty. Soon I felt good.

I kept thinking, I could really enjoy all this, under other circumstances.

And then thinking, Just be careful. Watch out.

Water wasn't, so far, a problem—there were lots of streams,

and I saw animals drinking from them, so they were nonpoiso-
nous. Of course, I didn't have any food beyond one sandwich.
But maybe I'd find recognizable berries or fruit or salads—the
Hulta had taught me quite a lot about food-things that grow
wild. But also again, I'm fairly used to going without food,
where I have to. The cruelty of the House, where a frequent
punishment was loss of meals, had taught me *that*.

The worst thing, obviously, was not knowing how far off
was this town called Panther's Halt. And what the rest of the
walk was going to be like. I mean, this forest was fine, but the
countryside might well change. Also, the *name* of the place now
bothered me rather.

I'd recalled something Ro and Mehmed had once talked
about. A forest "over north" with *panthers*. And—trees that
leaned down and grabbed people, wound them up in something (?), and then slowly digested them, over months—!

Unfortunately I began to think more and more about this.

By now I'd walked for hours, with one rest. The light was
deepening, thickening, and slanting in sidelong behind me,
making rich golden ponds on the narrow earth path. In other
words, it was getting near sunfall, and so nighttime. And even
the kindest woods can alter after dark.

Don't get feeble, Claidi. You can make a fire; you know how
to do that now; the Hulta taught you. And we'll sit by the fire
and drink the tea and eat half the sandwich, and then maybe
sleep. And besides, it won't *be* dark for at least another couple
of hours. . . .

Just then, I came out through a wall of birches and conifers
and saw that the forest was coming to an end.

The unnerving thing was, it really did just—end. A few more tall old trees, heavy with sun-struck foliage—and then this wide gap of only sky.

I marched forward, through the trees. And stopped. I had to. The land I was on had itself come to a stop. It was a cliff's edge. No way down, at least for me. The rock, though still green with shrubs and plants, seemed to drop more or less sheer to a plain far, far below. Yes, I know I tend to exaggerate, but it looked at least two hundred feet down.

(I've noticed, I think more in feet and yards now, more than I did before I was with Venn at the Rise. (Even being with Hrald and Yazkool, the two who kidnapped me—then vanished so weirdly—even with them I think I started to.) In the House I didn't bother much with those sort of measurements. With the Hulta, I picked up their way of saying man-heights (about six feet). Oh well. At least I used man-heights when I was shouting at Blurn.)

To get back to the point.

The cliff dropped down and down as I stood there, and my heart and stomach and spirits did the same. Down and down.

The land below looked empty and bare—but that wasn't my immediate concern.

What now?

Well, there was only one course. I'd have to pick along the side of the cliff, follow the forest edges along, until I came to a part where I could descend. I'm not going to try bravely to climb down. I'd make a mess of it and fall.

Anyway, I started to walk along the cliff top, going with the forest. I kept roughly about *one man-height* length from the edge, except where I had to cross back in a bit, around trees. I was wise to do that, because here and there, the cliff had crumbled. In one place a massive oak hung out across the gulf, some of its roots showing where the rock had given way.

The sky meanwhile melted from blue to violet.

The light of day soaked into the forest behind me. When I looked back, it was one moment all gilded red and jade-gold, and then it turned black, then ashen—then the light was gone. The forest became formless and dark.

That huge sky, hanging in a luminous sheet out there, will also go black soon. I can already see a few stars.

I've sat down and written this, and now I can hardly see what I'm writing in the light of the fire I made.

It's night.

Already I've heard weird sounds from the forest. I expect it's only owls or something.

Time to throw another branch on the fire. Or would it be better to get up a tree? Safer, that is.

Really it wasn't confidence or courage that made me fall asleep. I was tired. The dying of the firelight woke me, as I'd hoped it would, so I could build the protective blaze up again.

As I leaned over to push in more dry twigs, I saw the panther, sitting across the fire, looking at me.

My heart did what it does at such times. Stopped, then jumped with a jolt that shook me. I never find that very helpful.

Perhaps I made sound. A sort of stifled squawk, most likely.

The panther twitched its ears.

It was very black, its pelt like costly velvet. Its eyes were a silvery moon-yellow, but emerald where the fire caught in them.

How do I know how to identify a panther? I've seen pictures. Even on the Star I had looked at the picture of a panther in an interested way, because of the name of the town.

I now remembered the knife Dagger gave me. I eased it from the loop in my belt.

I thought, I can't kill a panther. I don't *want* to. And anyway, I've never learned to fight—

Then, the panther *spoke* to me.

Right, I've gone mad. No, it's a dream. It's a dream *and* I've gone mad.

The panther said, "Get up, follow. Come on, I will not wait."

Well, it was a dream, so why not?

Anyway, was I going to make a scene and *annoy* it?

I stood up.

The panther said, "Bring your luggage."

My—? Oh, it meant my bag. How thoughtful of it to remind me.

"Kick dirt over your fire," said the panther, evidently very responsible. "You will not be returning."

"Er—why not?" I nervously asked.

"I am to show you," said the panther, "the way down to the valley."

It had a cool, bored voice. Yes, it sounded bored. This was a nuisance for it, having to leave its normal panther-type activities, and come and help me down the cliff since I was too duppish to have figured out a way for myself.

I kicked leaf-mold and dirt over the fire.

[38]

Apparently not adequately, because the panther now stalked up—I shrank—and paw-brushed more stuff over it.

The moon was up, another panther eye in the sky.

"Ah—thanks."

"Follow me now," said the panther.

I can remember things in books about talking animals. They were always funny, or wise. This one just went on sounding matter-of-fact and *bored*.

It walked ahead of me, swinging its lean hindquarters, the velvet bell-rope of tail flicking from side to side.

"Mind the roots," it presently said, so I minded them. Felt I had to thank it again.

But when I stubbed my toe anyway, I thought, No, I'm not dreaming. This is real.

Next there were some very tall trees, and the panther walked in between, and when I did too, there was a hump of rock coming out of the cliff, a kind of chimneylike structure. In the side of it, a hole, or opening.

"There," said the panther.

"Yes?"

The panther shut its eyes. It looked—exasperated.

"Inside the rock is an entrance to caves that run through the cliff. Follow the slope downward, taking no side turnings. This will bring you to the valley floor."

"Right."

"Do not," said the panther, eyeing me sternly, "wait until daybreak. For then the bats return."

"I don't mind bats," I wildly confessed.

"However, they may not care for *you*."

"Ah yes, I see. Of course."

The panther gave me one long stare, then turned.

"Wait—" I heard myself (disbelieving I did) call.

"What do you want?"

"Look, I apologize for asking—but—how is it you can talk?"

"I might," said the panther, "ask you the same."

Shattered, I stood there gawking. Then I said, "Look—no, people do talk. But animals—don't."

"How do you know?"

"I don't *know* but—oh come on. Do they?"

"Generally, they do not."

"Then why is it—?" I began.

The panther turned again. It walked back toward me, and I wished I'd kept quiet.

It came so close, I felt the living heat of it, the muscular terrible strength. Its head was level with my ribs, but it was overall very much bigger than me, and heavy—yet *light*, sprung steel with a coat of plush. It smelled of night and darkness, and its breath stank of raw meat—the last thing it had killed and eaten.

"Claidi, who must always ask questions," said the panther.

"You know my name."

"You ask too much, but now is the time for action, not words."

My legs felt watery. On the other hand, my mouth was too dry to speak.

It gave me, the great black doglike cat, one last look of lingering disdain. And then it leapt around and bounded into the forest.

I tottered into the rock chimney. I leaned on the wall.

Then, by some trick of the outside moonlight, I glimpsed the curve of the wall, and a sloping stony track angling down.

I wandered onto it, started to descend. All the questions I hadn't asked were beating around and around in my head.

I realized a bit late why I could see my way. Clusters of fireflies were there, hanging like necklaces of topaz and green beryl, or dancing over pockets of water.

The ancient sinews of the stone arched overhead. Twisted trunks of stone strained up to hold them.

Everything reeked of the absent bats. And here and there the odd grape-bunch of bats was still hung up, having overslept or something.

Once one bat, a pale one, an albino, flew right at me. And as I ducked I thought, *What is it going to say?*

But the bat didn't speak, except maybe in battish, so luckily I hadn't a clue about it.

I was still so stunned that finally I sat down on the rim of a largish pool, where the dancing fireflies reflected like candles.

Some things have happened to me since I left the House. The Waste outside, I was always told, was full of bizarre and horrifying creatures. Though the House lied a lot, certain parts of the Waste—the world—are exactly what I was told they would be.

But no one warned me about talking panthers.

What can you do with something so curious and unsettling? Just shove it to the back of your mind, and carry on.

✦ ✦ ✦

I'd filled the by-then empty tea-bottle with water in the forest; there'd been a spring near my fire, with a squirrel drinking in the dusk. When I at last got out of the caves, I tried a sip. It tasted rather bitter, but all right. In fact it was.

The exit from the cliff was another cave, very wide and high, a great arch which showed plainly from inside, because by then it was getting on for dawn.

Apart from falling asleep again briefly by the pool, I had, it seemed, walked all night.

The bats were streaming home to bed as I moved out of the last cave. They passed over me, a chattering, soft yet spiky wind of shadows.

It was a cold morning.

It was dim; I still couldn't see much. But from above, the valley-plain had looked uninviting.

Wait for the sun. It should come up—over there.

By the cave-mouth I sat and dozed.

When I woke again, the sun was up, shining in my face.

The valley was what it had looked like. Arid slopes and hummocks, with sparse, dun-colored grass. One or two wan and spindly trees. Stones, boulders. No water I could see.

This muddled on to the horizon, and on the horizon there was nothing new.

Lovely.

All this to do on a small bottle of water, half a sandwich, three or four hours sleep.

Too bad. Ahead (somewhere) lay the town. With Zeera's house. And Argul. He would be there. He must be there. Or if not—someone who would know something.

In those books I read, a talking animal that guided you always did so for a good reason.

I allowed myself one chomp of the half-sandwich, and reduced it to a quarter-sandwich. Then I strode off east, toward the sun.

THE TENT

𝔄nyway, less than ten minutes later, I found a ROAD.

There was no doubt. It was even *paved*, if not very well. Along the sides grew a few more of the poor old trees. Coming around the slight upslope, I'd mistaken it at first for some natural gully. Fortunately went down and looked.

It wobbled off northeast, but soon there was a big rough-cut stone that read (in my own language, which I must *not* forget is also the language of the Towers), *Panther's Halt—Keep Right On.*

Also I hadn't been on it more than half an hour before some carts came bumbling along out of the wasteland and got onto the road about thirty yards ahead of me.

So far as I could see, there were three carts, all drawn by what looked like goats.

To begin with I was glad they were ahead, and I lagged back. In my experience, it isn't always sensible to trust one's fellow travelers.

Then I thought maybe they were all right, and might know something, so I quickened my pace.

As I got closer, I could see they were glancing back at me, even the goats were glancing back, but they made no effort to slow down.

There were three men and three women, and three goats. In the drab landscape they all wore very gaudy clothing, of reds and oranges, while the goats were black and white, or would have been, because somehow somebody had dyed their white parts, so the goats were black and puce, or black and aquamarine blue.

"Fine morning," I said, trying to sound and appear both harmless and well-armed, smashing good company and nobody's fool. Thinking about it, I suppose all the things I *totally* never am.

The carters looked me over, still not hesitating. One of the men said something, and it was in some other language. So I had to shrug and look ever so sorry—yet not concerned. (And also as if I might secretly understand—in case they were plotting something.) (I mean, *what*, for heaven's sake? Dying me blue and puce, perhaps. Well, you never know.)

Then one of the women leaned from her cart and said a couple of things in the other language. And then: "You go Panther's Halt, you do?"

"*Yes*," I exclaimed, all plots flung to the winds.

And I thought perhaps she would ask me to sit in the cart. But no such luck.

"You want goat?"

"A goat? Oh, no, thanks."

"Glamorous and work-good goat. See! In bestest color."

"No, thanks, really."

One of the men chipped in quickly, "We change the color if you want."

"No—no."

"Any color—merf, cashrob, coppice—*ranaky*, we do *ranaky* for you. Even horns we do!"

Why is it I *never* meet anyone normal?

Is it *me?*

"No goat," I said firmly. "*Thank* you."

At which they all, goats included, turned from me and refused to speak to me again during the rest of the trek to Panther's Halt. At least the *goats* didn't try any sales patter. After the panther, I'd half expected them to.

Not long after this episode, we went up quite a steep small hill, and from the top I could see, some way off, something blooming there on the dullness of the plain. It looked absurdly like a great, deep-pink flower.

"What is that?" I asked the goat-people.

But they wouldn't talk to me, so I had to wait to find out.

I don't think Argul ever was here before, or perhaps he was. . . . But Dagger wasn't, surely, or she'd have told me about this unusual—to me—town, Panther's Halt. Or are there lots of other towns just like it?

Panther's Halt is all under one vast *Tent*.

And not just any enormously vast tent, either. It is made of some special weatherproofed material and is raised at its top at least twenty feet higher than the roof of the tallest house on the tallest hill up there, inside the town. Standing in the streets of the Halt, you look up and see these higher streets and buildings tapering up into the cyclamen-pink dome of the Tent. It's like being under an always-blushing dawn.

There are millions of tiny holes made in the material, secured by thin rings of some metal which, it seems, can't rust. (?) Through these ringed holes faint musical whinings of breezes blow, and the very occasional single spot of rain. But as a rule, the Tent keeps off all weather, including the searing midday sun, which otherwise burns and drains the valley.

Inside the Tent, trees grow on the streets. They're still pastel but quite luxuriant.

At night, lamps will apparently come on, far up in the canopy of the Tent. So that even at night, the blush-dawn effect will continue.

These lamps never have to be lit or put out. At night they light, at sunrise they darken. They have a soft clear radiance, which doesn't flicker. Familiar? They're exactly like the lamps at the Rise. *Ustareth's* lights.

Is that really so surprising?

She has this house here, Dagger said.

Did Ustareth-Zeera therefore arange the lights and the town's Tent?

Around the edges of the town, just outside the Tent, are canals, into which any moisture or rain, which collects on the Tent-top, is eventually dislodged.

After heavy storms, or when there is a buildup of water on

the Tent-top, there is a Rope-Shaking Brigade, who go outside and shake the ropes fixed between the ground and the upper Tent, and so knock off the water. The Brigade is highly respected. They wear a uniform—black, with Tent-pink epaulets and buttons, and black-lacquered helmets to protect them when they shake the water down to the canals.

The canals are additionally full of ducks. The ducks, plus thousands of other birds, come in and out of the town by means of folded-back openings kept wide by day. Lots of birds perch along a sort of scaffolding which in places upholds the Tent from inside.

I have a language problem here.

Despite the stone on the road, not many people speak mine. They do speak a bit of Hulta, which I've learned rather haphazardly. (I know a lot of Hulta swearing, and affection-words, and even whole songs, and lots of whole sentences—but, well, I was only really starting to get properly to grips with it when— when I was taken away.)

But it's not too bad. Just—oh, completely frustrating. I simply haven't been able to ask about Argul, because I haven't the words. Not even about U-Z's house, which is almost certainly where he is staying, if he is here.

I've been wandering the streets all day, too tired now to feel anything but violently alert and awake, too hungry to want to eat. But I'm thirsty.

They have these fountains here. They are on almost every street, and in the big square, where there is a market, there are four. The sparkling water gushes over them, and on each, in several different languages—including mine—are these big black words: DO NOT DRINK.

At first I thought it was just nastiness. Then I realized the water may look all right, but it's probably *not* drinkable, poisonous even. (I am sitting by a fountain now, writing this, and it's driving me nuts.)

I'm thinking of going out again to the canals for a drink. Full of ducks and duck feathers, not to mention little parcels of ducky doo.

Of course, I have no money. And they use money here. Also barter—but I have nothing I can afford to let go. I'm walking around with a diamond ring and an embroidered Hulta wedding dress in my bag, and I have a honed blade through my belt. But these are the most precious things in my life.

I've done this all wrong.

Without any difficulty, I'd say, Yinyay could have found me some money notes, or something marketable, before she shrank. Didn't think to ask. Or even search.

How typical.

Serves me right then.

Oh, there goes another goat. Black and pea-green. Very tasteful.

(Those goat people must have brought them to sell them, and when I came belting after them, thought I wanted to buy one quickly. So they weren't as dotty as I reckoned. Though they *were* rude.)

And *another* goat—black and pink, like the Rope-Shakers. (An old man told me about the Rope-Shakers, in halting Hulta, after some of the Brigade swaggered by. A passing girl also told me about the lamps, seeing me staring up at them in the Tent top. Possibly they just have these sightseer sentences ready-prepared in many languages.)

There are no horses for sale in the market.

When I said (in Hulta), "Horses?" to someone, just to see, this person laughed. I *think* he replied, *sold out.*

No panthers either. Not that I've noticed.

I *am* tired. I'd like to lie down and sleep somewhere quiet. And I'm thirsty enough to drink a bath full of pooey duck-water. And really I'm starving.

This room's all right. The woman warned me I'd be woken by the noise of the morning market starting under my window. But I didn't wake. I must have slept from late afternoon yesterday until the same today.

I feel much better. I can think more clearly. Which is a shame, in a way, because now I can really worry.

And the worst thing of all? In order to get this room in this inn, and a meal and so on—I sold my wedding dress. Do you think I'm beneath contempt? I feel very, very bad about it.

What happened was, I was sitting by that fountain, when this man came up. He looked rather like the goat-people in dress, but then he thrust his face into mine and squinted at me with his narrow little eyes.

"What you selling?"

"I beg your pardon?"

"What you selling? Great strong girl like you—" somehow

he made this sound insulting, as if I were extremely tall and beefily heavy and loud—"come on, come on. I'll hire you."

"For what?" I said.

I felt threatened, and although there were plenty of people about, I didn't know whether they'd care if I got attacked.

"Well," said the repulsive man, "you can clean up. Do the washing. Cook the supper. How's that?"

"No, thank you ever so much."

But he leered, He reminded me of certain servants, and even the occasional royal person at the House, who I'd always tried to keep well clear of.

"Come on," he said. "You might get to like me."

"You're very nice. But I'm waiting for someone."

Then he swelled like a toad, got even fatter and uglier, and I put my unskilled hand on the dagger in my belt. And then someone else leaned over *him*, and dragged him bodily away, as if he were a bag of rubbish, and just sort of threw him casually down several feet off.

"Leave the lady alone," said the new someone.

I thought there might be a fight. But instead the first man was groveling there on the ground. "Sorry, sorry," he was mumbling, "didn't know she was with you—"

The newcomer said, "She's not." Then he turned to me and gave me a jaunty salute.

He was tall, thin, and dry for the other one's oily, stout shortness. Not young, or old. A black stubble of hair crowned his head. He wore creaky black leather.

"Are you here on business, madam?" he politely asked.

I got up. He *towered* over me. But he spoke my language (so had the other one, alas) so I said, "No, I'm here looking for someone."

"And who is that?"

"Well—" cautious now, I added, "for their house, really."

"A house." He gave me a dry thin smile. His skin looked like that paper you can sand things down with. "I regret, I'm a stranger here myself."

And then he *bowed* and walked off. Couldn't help noticing, people got out of his way.

To my dismay the other one came gobbling back at once. But he only wanted to say, "Sorry, dear. Sorry. Didn't know, miss, you knew Jelly."

Then he too hurried off.

Jelly.

At Peshamba I saw *jellies* served for the children. They'd been set in exotic molds and had come out in the shapes of rabbits and lions and stars and suns, and all in jewel-like colors. Happy party food.

Jelly???

Still, it had been lucky he was there.

I decided then I'd better get sorted out, before anything else happened. And I went straight over to a booth that was selling clothes, some of which were clearly secondhand.

Without letting myself think, I produced the embroidered wedding dress. "What will you give me for this?" I didn't know if they understood—they seemed to understand what I was trying to do at least. "It's a family heirloom. Hardly worn. I know it's stained. That's from a long sea voyage, therefore interesting. The embroidery is Hulta."

They gave me coins and rushed my WD away behind the booth, so I was fairly sure I'd been done.

I've felt horrible about it ever since, even dreamed about it, I think, during the deep sleep in this inn-room.

But I still have the diamond ring. I'm not confident enough to wear it after the thing with the rings, at the Rise. I don't know what powers it has—and they're erratic. But I would *never* sell it. Even though, before she gave it to Argul, it was *hers*. Ustareth-Zeera.

Now I'm up, washed (even hair), have had some breakfast-lunch. I'm going to find that house today.

Wonder how Yinyay is managing in the storage of the Star—learning things, did she say? I wonder too how Venn is, all across the ocean. And Jotto and Treacle and Grem.

And Argul. How and where are you?

Really, I think I was just certain by now I wasn't going to find Argul at Panther's Halt. That the best I could hope for was a clue.

Why was this? I'd suspected I would *feel* something electric in the air of the Tent town, if he had been here too. Then—I *had* felt that, sort of—but didn't trust what I felt.

The already-late day got later as I trudged around the streets. They were paved, but hilly. And also the paving was fairly cracked and rather unsafe. Yesterday I hadn't seen the lights come on; I'd been asleep. But now, as the daylight through the under-Tent began to fade, suddenly the lamps opened their cool eyes, and everything went pinker than ever.

The birds were flying in to their scaffolding roosts, tweeting and trilling. No doubt the lights also help keep them warm during the cold nights. Trails of birds arrowed and darted under the pink dome "sky." Droppings fell like white streamers, and people dashed to gather them in little pots(??).

Between dodging droppings, I was trying to get a look at all the bigger houses on hill tops. Wouldn't *her* house be one of these? A commanding view of the town, and so on. Then again, she might have wanted a concealed house, tucked away in a big garden of thick bushy trees.

I had just reached the wall of such a garden. A wide gate stood open, and down a long coiling path I could now see another sort of light among the shrubbery. Paper lanterns, rose, crimson, blue. There was the sound of merrymaking and clink of glasses and jugs.

"Why, hallo again," said a dry voice behind me. "What a coincidence. Are you too going to the goat-wedding?"

I jumped around—hadn't heard a step or anything—and there he was. Jelly.

"The—what did you say?"

"Goat-wedding. Shall we?" He bowed, as he had before. Something about the bow—it's what they do for royalty in the Houses and the Towers.

Had he followed me?

Was I only being oversensitive?

But he'd put his hand courteously under my elbow, and we were walking into the garden. As if on a long-arranged outing.

"Let me introduce myself," he said. "I am Jelly."

"Hi." (His hand was icy. I was glad when he removed it.)

"And you?"

"Oh." Efficient as ever, I hadn't thought beforehand I might not want to give my name to everyone. So I hadn't prepared a fake name, and for a moment I dithered.

"If I am being too forward, there's no need to say, naturally," he assisted me, sounding now indescribably threatening and sinister.

An idea surfaced. Chancy—but let me see how he took it.

"Of course I can tell you my name. It's Ustareth," I announced.

And he stopped dead. His long thin face stared down at me, all chin, and even the *chin* looked *interested*.

"*Uss*-taar-eth," he intoned. His pouchy eyes glittered. "What a fascinating name."

"Thank you so much," I gushed.

"A City name, I think," he said. "The City on the River, surely. From a Tower?"

"Wouldn't know," I said. "My mum thought it up."

"Your mother *thought it up?*"

"Oh, they all used to laugh in my village," I rambled on, unwisely warming to my game. "Bat's Junction Village. You know it? No? I thought everyone had heard of Bat's Junction. Anyway, they used to tease me rotten."

"How trying," he said.

He seemed to like this too, and that chilled me down. Games—he liked games—the Towers like games. The Wolf Tower.

He is from the Wolf Tower? From *Ironel—*

"*Your* name is so much more interesting," I twittered. "*Jelly—*"

"Oh let's not talk about me."

We were in among the paper lanterns now, and the noisy crowd was falling back from us, cheery faces going all tense as they registered *him*.

"I believe you said you were looking for someone's house?" he now asked me.

"Did I?"

"I'm sure you did."

"Oh yes, that's right. The house of my mother's cousin—"

"And who is that?"

Hell, another name to think up on the spur of the moment.

"Pattoo," I uncleverly blurted, picking the name of a friend from my slave-maid days.

"All this is most interesting," said Jelly. He strolled beside me. "I wonder if," he said, "on your travels about the town, and in the house of your mother's cousin Pattoo—if you have come across a young woman by the name—" he paused. An abrupt shouting and music burst all around.

For a moment I had the feeling he had seen something that had startled him, broken off to check this something out—but then I realized.

He was playing.

He's standing there, and he's going to say *Claidi*. Or Claidis or Claidissa. Those name changes the Wolf Tower gave me.

Cat and mouse. And I'm the mouse.

I waited, gaping at the crowd all breaking apart in a dancing procession, with high-held torches and bottles and garlands of gold tinsel flowers.

Waited, not really seeing anything, *waited* to hear him speak that name—

Only he didn't.

I couldn't bear another second. I turned to confront him, this—Jelly—

He was gone.

Vanished. He'd just slid away among the shadows of the garden as if on wheels.

Idiotically I looked back at the festivity.

And here came the bride.

She was a goat.

I frowned, but no, she was. How then did I know her to be the bride? Easy. She wore my own Hulta wedding dress.

The evil Jelly was gone, and now the crowd was pushing into and around me, so I gave up and was also carried along through the garden. And so I was next able to watch the wedding. If the bride was a surprise, the groom was more of a surprise.

Like before, a chatty old woman soon came up and started to tell me what went on, in my own language, more or less. Is it worth recording? Yes, I suppose it is.

The goat in (my) wedding dress, was one of the black and green ones. They "married" her to a panther. This was lighter in color than the one that had spoken to me in the forest. You could, in the light, see the paw-print pattern in his coat.

"Have no feary," said the old woman. "The panther do no harm to the goat. We train they panthers here to live with goats as family. And they goat-people train their goaties same. See now, they making the friends."

This was a fact? The goat and the panther were standing and leaning on each other, all relaxed. Now and then the panther rubbed its head, like a big cat, on the goat. The goat was so calm, it was grazing the grass.

"In us valleys," said the old woman, "they panther do be guardy goaties herds. None so safe as they."

(I'm only jealous. I wish I could speak another language even as well as she was speaking mine.) (Then again, though, she wasn't really.)

Desperate, I rounded on her.

"A woman called Zeera," I hissed, "or Ustareth—her house—do you know where it is?"

She giggled at me. "Juppa yipto?"

"You don't really speak my language at all, " I accused. "It's just this sightseer stuff you've learned by heart, isn't it?"

She beamed. She inquired, helpfully, "You like a goat?"

As I hurried away from her, I saw, across the red flap of the torches, lit as I had so often seen him, by fire, Argul, standing on the slope above.

LIGHT OR DARK?

Had he seen *me?*

I didn't think so. He was looking down at the bridal procession which was now swirling around again, weaving about every tree—

Had he seen the *dress* on the goat? The dress that had been going to be mine on the day I should have married *him?*

I remember saying, when I first met Argul—I was afraid of him. He was just so absolute. So *entire*, complete.

And now, as the bouncing crowd pushed me back and forth, staring up at him on the lawn above, again I was afraid.

I'd forgotten what he truly looks like.

Under the shift of firelight, his dark skin one instant like bronze, and then like gold. His black hair that hangs to his waist. His face—his face.

Another panther, with two or three goats—bridesgoats and Best Panther, perhaps—thumped into me. I was toppled back good-naturedly against a tree by the crowd.

Then the crowd was past, rioting off through the garden toward the town, and I got my bearings—but I'd looked away one whole thin-as-a-splinter second. And in that second, Argul had moved.

I was in time to catch the flare of his brown cloak, crack of one golden inch of tassel-fringe, as he strode away into the trees above.

All the time I'd spent asking myself: When I find him, how am I going to approach him, what am I going to say to him?— Of course I was simply pelting up the garden, and now I was yelling his name.

But there was still a lot of noise, not least from the wedding orchestra of squeaky trumpets and throaty drums.

He hadn't heard me, couldn't have.

I ran.

On the upper lawn, the trees divided to form an avenue. Again, I was just in time to see him striding along it.

Rushing through the avenue. He is around the next turn before I get there. I mustn't lose him. *Mustn't.*

At the turn, there is a hill. Argul is striding up the hill. How far ahead of me? Quite a lot. I stop and try yelling his name again.

But the night seems full of distant calls and songs. To him, so far ahead of me now, my cry will sound only like one more of these.

Argul, wait. Please wait. Stop for something—spot an interesting rare type of owl perched on a tree or a pole above—catch your cloak on a briar—hesitate because some memory has come into your mind—some memory of me—

No good. I start running again.

He is at the top of the hill—for a moment in silhouette against the bright-lit Tent dome. Look around, Argul, look back—here I am—

He doesn't. He's going on over the hill, down the hill.

Running uphill isn't my favorite mode of travel. Have a stitch. No breath to shout. Long knotty grass. Now I've stumbled, tripped. More or less fall over, scramble up, tear on, ignoring another prize-winning knee-bruise to add to my knee-and-elbow bruise collection—

As I splurled over the hilltop, I had this nightmare feeling he would simply have disappeared. And he had. He had.

I dropped on the slightly less bruised knee.

Try not to go mad. Think. What is down there? See, it's obvious. A paved path goes down to those houses over there, and it's quite well lit from the Tent lights, though they seem a little dimmer here. If he were walking on the path, I'd still see him.

But first there is that single building, tucked in among those cypress trees. Darker there. It must be—*that* is the house, and he has gone into it.

And exactly then, a lamp burns up yellow in one window which seems caught in the boughs of a cypress tree.

I leapt to my feet—

"Felt like a bit of a run, did you?"

—and nearly plummeted right off the hill.

Now I was so unnerved, frenzied, no pretense seemed worth the effort.

I whirled on him.

It *was* Jelly.

"Are you following me?"

"Am I? Hmn."

"Get lost," I barked.

"Tut tut. But where are you sprinting to in such a hurry? Tell me, madam, have you ever run professionally? My word, swift as a gazelle."

"What's a gaz—*look*, Jelly, what do you want?"

"Ah. So many things. A little cottage by a trout pool. A reasonable wine-cellar—"

"Who do you think I am?" I challenged.

"You told me," he said. "Ustareth."

"You say you're a stranger here," I said, "but they all seemed to know you."

"Word gets around."

"Which word?"

"My name. Jelly," he said, modestly.

I wasn't going to go down to the cypress house until Jelly was gone. Right now, I didn't dare even look at the house except quickly, once. The light still burned. As if to be my beacon.

"Wolf Tower," I said to Jelly. "Yes?"

"Ah?" asked Jelly, rolling innocent pouchy razor-sharp eyes.

No one else was around. The garden—park, really—was deserted here. And the Tent lights, as I said, were not so bright from this point.

If it came to it, I didn't think I could get the better of this man with a dagger.

How to get rid of him?

Now he bent down and down to me. (He must be nearly seven and a half feet tall.)

"Tell me, madam, you *are* the Lady Claidis Star, aren't you?"

"Who?"

"Claidis Star. Who goes more often by the pet name of Claidissa. Or even . . . Claidi."

"My name's Ust—"

"Good night," said Jelly.

I stood there, mouth open. There he went, off back down the hill, the way we had both come. (His walk, seen from a distance, is extraordinary. At every step he bends at the knees, and yet he covers vast amounts of ground on his enormous feet, like a sort of power-driven spider.)

I descended the other slope, very slowly and carefully now, keeping clear of trees, looking back again and again. I anticipated every moment he'd rearrive: "Oh, before I go—"

But he didn't.

Below, I hung around for ages. No one about. Yet I had this awful sense that Jelly, if he meant to, could still creep up on me, unseen, unheard.

Roosting birds stirred nearby, had a little singsong, and went back to sleep.

I crept among the cypress trees.

Somehow this was like her other house (Ustareth's) on the lake, when I was with Venn.

And the light above me, that was like that other time with

Venn, under that room of his in the gardens of the Rise, look-ing up at his lighted window in the dark, lost and friendless, knowing him to be my enemy.

Argul isn't my enemy. But—he thinks I am his.

It took a while for me to get my courage together and knock on the carved door under the arch.

I kept thinking it *would* have been far simpler to have gal-loped up to him screaming.

Obviously I hadn't knocked loudly enough. There was no answer.

So I beat with both fists, boldly. The night seemed to shake, and oddly, nearby, one of those duller lights overhead went out, as if I'd damaged it by making a row.

It was black now, or seemed to be, in the cypress grove.

Still no one answered.

Then I knocked and called. Then I went and stood under the lighted window. And after all that, I yelled again!

The lamp was behind a filmy curtain. I couldn't see what was in the room.

Perhaps he'd left the lamp, forgotten. Gone to another room.

I walked around the house, here and there having to go up steps or crawl over low walls with extra thorns. I shouted and called, using his name. I even threw a couple of small stones to rattle the glass window panes.

Some while after, I sat under a bush.

Then I tried to *break* into the house.

But I'm useless at that sort of thing, and nothing would give; the only windows I could reach were locked. Didn't want to smash them. I mean, Hi, Argul, here is the vile horror you think ran off with another man without even telling you, and now I'm back, and I've just broken your window, too.

I did climb up a tree. After all, it was a shame not to add cuts and grazes to the bruises and thorn-scratches. I tried to crane over and bang on the lighted window. Couldn't *reach*.

I did a bit more calling and shouting, and right then, a band of six or seven young men came along the path toward the hill and waved up at me delightedly. "Look, lads, it's a foreign female mad person!"

Colossal laughter and congratulations to me. (Please note, the words were carefully spoken in *my* language.)

When they had at last gone on again, I did think at least their noise must have woken Argul—but it hadn't.

Then I thought, He isn't sleeping. He has either seen or heard me. He knows it's me, out here. And out here is where he means me to remain.

Later, much later, a panther and goat trotted by together under my cypress tree. Friends for life.

Argul, if a panther and a goat can be friends—surely you could at least listen to me, hear me out.

But in my head, I heard a voice that answered, He is doing to you what he thinks you did to him. Misled and made a fool of him. Used and lied to him. Left him out in the cold.

If he could unbelievably abandon the Hulta because of what he thought I'd done, then what do *I* matter to him now?

He must hate and loathe me.

By the yellow glow of the lamp (*his* lamp), I've written this.

Another overhead light has gone out. They must be faulty

here. Is there any connection between this and Ustareth's Star-ship developing a fault and crash-landing?

Shall I tear a page out of this book and write him a letter? Saying what?

Maybe it's all I can do. But it's harder to see to write, even his lamp is burning low. I'll have to wait until daybreak. I might as well stay up in this tree. It may be safer up here. If only from Jelly.

Morning. The overhead lights all went out in one blink, and a grey predawn turned the Tent top amethyst.

In this eerie dusk, I rubbed my cricked neck and almost fell out of the tree.

Below me, a young man was there at the front of the house. He led a horse, saddled up and ready for riding. A brown, satiny horse, strong as a tiger—

The door opened. Argul came out into the cold first light that smelled of cypresses, birds, and Tent.

If they spoke, I didn't hear the words. He just walked over to the horse and mounted up, swinging into the saddle as if weightless, the way I'd seen him do so many times now my heart seemed to dissolve. There was a carrying bag, too, fixed on behind the saddle.

I'd only been building up my breath and throat. Now I shrieked at him.

The *other* man's head shot up all right; he nearly sprang out of his skin. But Argul didn't even look my way.

Though I heard him speak. To the man.

"Noisy birds you get here."

"Yeah—" said the other, stunned.

Argul touched the horse lightly. He was riding away. Then he was racing away.

I fell down the tree.

Trying to run after Argul, my knees gave.

"Morning," said the young man as I landed at his feet. "Legs not so strong as your lungs, eh?"

I realized he was speaking in Hulta.

Hulta phrases spun in my head.

"Argul—where's he going?"

"You know Argul?"

I nodded vigorously until my head seemed about to fly off.

"Shame he didn't realize it was you," said the young man. "He's off north. Over the burning Fiery Hills."

"Horse—" I burbled, in Hulta. Of all Hulta words, that word is anyway the first anyone ever learns.

"Yes, Argul's is a great horse."

"No—no—me—I want—horse—"

"Can't have it, luv," said the young man. "It's *Argul's* horse."

Shall I just kill him?

No. Keep trying.

(*He* saw me. *He* knew me. He doesn't *want* me. I don't care. Until I have convinced him of the truth—then I can allow him only to decide. It may still go against me. I'll worry then. Die, then.)

"For me—a—a *new* horse."

Had I said *new?* Thinking back, I think I said a *fat* horse. In Hulta, the words are similar.

But at last this pest got my drift.

"Oh, you won't get a horse now. Sold out last cow-day."
(I *think* he said *cow*-day.) "Tell you what, though, my dad can
probably fix you up with a riding animal—not a horse, but
something."

"Anything." What else could I say? (Only actually, I may
have said, not anything, but any *gherkin.*)

ACROSS THE FIRE HILLS
BY GRAFFAPIN

This creature is *not* a horse. But the burning Fiery Hills *do* burn. They flame. Yet, to be fair, they are not on fire, as such. They look spectacular, particularly after sunset.

The graffapin doesn't look spectacular. It looks peculiar.

It's like a horse slightly. That is, the back is broad enough and the legs muscular enough so you can ride it. No real tail. The neck goes straight up—and up. I measured the neck, and it's the length of my arm from shoulder to wrist. Then comes the head, which isn't horselike either. More sheeplike. Big dark eyes, with *lashes*. Two upstanding ears. All of it covered with dripping long blond fur—or pelt—or fleece—or hair.

It smells insistently of damp hay, despite the grooming it had at Panther's Halt.

"Does it have a name?" I'd uneasily asked.

"Graff," said "Dad"—that was all the name *he* had, that I heard.

Graff cost very little, or rather, the coins I'd been given for my WD (now fashionable goat-wear) were worth more than I'd thought (so they hadn't ripped me off).

Supplies were thrown in, plus some food for the graffapin called Graff.

I don't even know if it's a girl or a boy—and apparently that's quite hard to discover.

It mutters to itself as we trot along, low gurgles and snuffles. But it goes fast when you say *Yof-yof.*

They warned me about the Hills.

Oh, ever so funny, silly foreign woman who looks upset when they tell her the hills are on fire all the time.

I didn't see them until two days' ride from the Tent and Panther's Halt. Graff was galloping, because although I'd been told by "Dad" that Argul would take the only decent road which I "couldn't miss," I was petrified of missing both road and Argul.

So then, it was getting on for sunset, and I thought these upper slopes were just catching the westering sun. Couldn't quite see how, as they faced me, therefore south.

As the light ebbed, the hills got brighter. Then I had to admit what "Dad" and his son had told me was presumably a fact.

It was night by the time Graff and I rode up to them. And sure enough, there was the road, another badly paved mess but still just about intact. On either side, fluttering and flickering, and lighting the lower sky like copper, the flames flashed and rippled.

They are red, with roots of saffron and fierce blue. No smoke rises—a giveaway.

"Dad" had said it was a "chemical reaction" and wouldn't hurt. Not fire at all, said Dad, proud of his superior knowledge and living in such a pride-worthy, eccentric area.

I wondered if the graffapin would take fright, throw me and bundle off. It just ambled up onto the road and trotted along, its fur-drippery shining as if it had on an expensive fringed tablecloth.

I stared.

Finally we made camp on the road, which is broad. I didn't light a fire, as the chemical fire gives off some warmth and is very bright.

As I was eating my supper, Graff managed to get out of his/her tether—he/she is very good at that, something to do with the long, twisting neck—and wandered off among the fires, puffing and admiring them, like a lady in a flower garden.

Despite appearances, Graff did not catch alight. Nor I, when I went after and hauled he/she/it back out.

But there is no sign of Argul.

Six days and nights now, since I left P H.

I said to Dad and son, what lay over the Fire Hills? And they pulled a face—they both pulled the same face at the same time. Anything beyond the Halt doesn't matter and/or is bad?

"But where is Argul going?"

"North."

"What is in the north?"

After some thought, Dad said, "It's bloody cold."

✦ ✦ ✦

Startling wildness of fire today, flaring up and up.

No animals or birds, except once, large black birds went over—ravens?

Still no Argul.

Am I on the wrong road? Are there two—three others—or has he just gone elsewhere—even asked or paid Dad and son to lie to me?

Please don't let that be so.

This morning, eighth day, I was high up. I saw Argul ahead.

My wonder and relief were slightly spoiled by *also* seeing another rider behind me. From the unbelievable look of him, it is *Jelly.*

That night I found a cave and went and sat in it, with Graff tied up very securely to a rock inside. If I went to sleep, I didn't want Jelly happening along and surprising me again. He had seemed quite a way behind me—but with Jelly, who could be sure?

He didn't come by. Or if he did, nothing woke me. (I had tied some of Graff's spare tether across the cave entrance, so anyone trying to get in would get tangled up with Graff and cause some noise.)

Graff, though, is such a peaceful beast. He—maybe he is a he—was just quietly singing to himself when I got up. I put on his nose-bag for him, and he sang his uncomplaining way through breakfast.

"Yof-yof!"

Off we briskly went.

I felt I must try to reach Argul now. Catch up with him. Yesterday, up ahead on the next piece of the hills, he had seemed to be traveling steadily but not fast.

One thing about a graffapin, or this one, it can really run, and *keep* running. Finally I had to say *Frum-froff*—the command to slow him down, because I'd realized he'd been haring along for about fifty minutes at around eighty miles an hour.

He didn't seem out of breath. Just started to gubble and snuffle to himself again, which, when going flat out, he hadn't.

No sign of Jelly today, but the lay of the land has no doubt just hidden him. He could be anywhere. Even riding *beside* me over there, somewhere, concealed by the high hill-shoulder and the fires.

And I haven't caught up to Argul. Or seen him again.

The road is worse. Whole bits missing.

Passed a fire-fountain, a cascade splashing over from some tall rocks, green-shot red.

"Are you still singing, Graff? You're a good boy."

Of course, I've begun to ask myself, did *she* (Ustareth) breed these animals, these graffapins, one more experiment, some unthinkable cross between—what? A horse, just maybe, and a sheep. . . ?(!)

And yes, I have thought about the panther I met in the forest, the talking one. I recall the people around the Rise, girls with flowers growing alive in their hair, and the woman who had two voices, one human, and the other all different birds' songs going at once.

A talking beast. Ustareth (Zeera): could she have managed that?

[73]

Sunset, and there's no handy hiding place tonight, no caves. The fires light everything up, including me.

I had a rest and a walk up and down, and some of the boring journey food. Now I'm going to mount Graff and go on, sleep in the saddle if necessary, use the night to travel. Perhaps I can catch up with Argul that way.

Jelly is on a horse. I assume it's the one he rode on into PH, as PH was "sold out." I had a chance to admire Jelly's horse, since they came galloping up to me in the black and moonless depth of the night.

"As we're both going the same way," said Jelly, friendly, "I thought we might as well travel together. What do you say?"

What I said was a Hulta swear-word used, even by Badger, Ro, and Mehm, only now and then. A curse you really do save for best (or worst).

Then I yowled *Yof-yofff* . . . and off we yoffed. Heaven bless lovely Graff, who inside two minutes had outraced the horse—already tired from racing after me—and kept on going.

"*Good* Graff—wonderful *handsome* Graff!"

Everything whizzed by in a whirlwind of fires and stars and fluttering graff-fluff.

We were speeding uphill, up and up, and I had a vague idea this might be unwise, we might hit the sky—or just plunge over some steep place at the top—when the hill flattened out and everything went jet black.

"*Frum-froffy-frum*—oh, whoah!"

Graff careened to a halt, and I nearly came off.

What had happened?

Something totally normal, so *naturally* utterly unlooked-for. We'd reached the end of the fires.

In front, the plateau ran away to the dark sky. And everywhere else the land poured over into the shadow of an ordinary night.

For a few minutes I sat there, getting my bearings, getting used to the dark. And I hoped Jelly too would come thundering up here and get thrown.

And then I saw there was one fire left, a small one, over there under that tumble of stones. Some outpost of the bigger fires? It looked like a campfire. . . .

Had I—was it—

I clicked my teeth at Graff, who trotted on. Time had stopped. And in the timelessness we reached the stones and came around them.

The fire was straightforward fire-color and set inside a ring of smaller stones. Nothing was roasting over it, spitting and smelling appetizing. I'd have expected there would be. Like me, he must already have eaten.

The brown horse was grazing the unburning turf. Argul sat against the wall of stones.

The fire caught in his eyes. Was it only that which made them so hard and brilliant, like black windowpanes, *closed?*

I dismounted, and he sat, watching me.

No pretense now. And no greeting.

"Argul?"

I stood in front of him, across the fire.

Soon he looked away with a terrible little smile. (Venn disturbed me so, resembling Argul so much. And now, the other way—Argul—is so like *Venn*.)

"Claidi." Said Argul, complete with a period.

In the tone he used, the voice he used, my name became a smear of dirt upon a distant path, long, long, ago.

"I know what you think."

"I'm sure you do. Even you, Claidi, aren't so dumb you wouldn't know that."

We had always been insulting to each other. Part of our play. Never *never* meant. Love and respect. Not anymore.

"Argul," I took a step forward, not realizing I had, and he said, "Stay that side of the fire. Maybe a shock to you, I don't want you near me."

"Right. Look, here I am. But will you let me tell you—" I wavered, had thought he would interrupt—"what really happened? It's not what you think."

"Suppose I don't care."

"If you knew the truth—"

Was this, after all, the hardest thing I'd ever faced? Dealing with enemies is bad enough, but an enemy who was a friend, someone I'd loved, still loved—

"Argul, I *have* to explain."

And then, right then, Jelly rode up. Having not been thrown at all—or made any noise I heard.

I only knew because Argul glanced up from that deep other place he was gazing down into because he didn't want to look at me. His eyes fixed beyond me, and he got to his feet.

"Mate of yours?" he asked softly.

"If he's about eight feet tall with black stubble hair, riding a vicious-looking blackish horse—no."

"My lord, my lady," called Jelly, bowing in the saddle, "what a stroke of good fortune."

Argul came past and around me. His cloak brushed over my arm. I shivered.

Jelly sat there, smiling his dry split of a smile.

"Why have you been following me?" I demanded.

"Because I hadn't yet caught up with you," outlined Jelly, with intelligent reasonableness.

"You know what I mean. You're from the Tower, aren't you? Who sent you? How did you trace me? There's no Tag on me now, none in my book—*was it Ironel Novendot?*"

Jelly was busy looking at Argul. Jelly's narrow eyes were knife-edged slits. He was concentrating.

Argul said, "I don't think she wants your company."

"I don't," I agreed.

Jelly widened his pouchy eyes to glinting slots.

Just then, I noticed he had a rifle slung over his shoulder. And Argul—didn't have one.

"This is the famous Argul, is it," said Jelly. "Leader of the Bandit Hulta Horse-People. Most pleased to meet you, my lord."

Argul said nothing.

Jelly, to my added horror, swung crankily off his horse.

"I have," said Jelly, looking now over at me, "something for you."

"What?"

"I've been looking for the right moment to give it to you."

"*What?*"

"This does not seem, much, the right moment."

Argul said, "Get back on your horse and go."

(Jelly, at eight feet, was taller than Argul.)

"That would be easier, wouldn't it?" nodded Jelly.

"But then. Know why they call me Jelly?" he asked me casually, looking at me past Argul now. (No one eagerly asked Why? Why?) Jelly said, "You were correct. Wolf Tower. The Wolf Tower molded me *like* a jelly, into the form and type I now am. I am a jelly of the Wolf Tower, and I am all *set.*"

Was this amusing, absurd, or ultra ghastly? Before I could decide, Argul took two strides. It happened so fast. Argul's fist crashed up into Jelly's middle, and Jelly made a noise and tilted. Then Argul's second fist hit Jelly square on the jaw, just like in a book.

Jelly spun, turned around as if about to march away, and fell splat, flat on his face. Didn't stir.

"Oh," I said, with my usual display of flawless wit. Felt slightly sick, actually.

"Get on that thing you're riding," said Argul. He was already in the saddle.

I ran to Graff, scrambled aboard.

As we tore off along the plateau, over its crest and down the other side in darkness, I cried out inside myself—*We're together now—*

But some minutes further on, when the pace slowed, Argul, riding at my side, said this:

"You can talk to me later, if you must. I don't want to hear it; it won't change anything. For now, shut up and listen. I'm going into the North. I'll take you to the town there. Then you are on your own. That's it. And Claidi . . ."

"Yes," I whispered.

"If you start yattering, or if you put one finger on me, you're on your own here and now. Keep your distance. And keep quiet until I tell you."

He is no longer like himself, at least with me. He sounds now like Venn at his worst, or like—Nemian. He sounds like the *others*, the *Wolf Tower*. (He has their blood. I never remember—he too—*he*—is Ironel's grandson.) Have *I* done this to him—made him into a monster, at least in my company? Yes, it's me. My fault.

WINTER

Once there used to be seasons. They were called, I think, spring, summer, fall-of-leaf, and winter. As the desert areas grew and the weather altered and became erratic, seasons more or less ended, as such. Sunny days can be followed by gales, and frosts by months of scorchers. Leaves are always falling off and at the same time new ones growing, fruits and blossoms can appear together, or else trees may stay bare for years. (Or else do things like sprouting froth.)

In the North, however, winter *is*. As you get near, they call it that. They even say, "Are you going on right to Winter, then? Then you'll need to buy this fur-lined jacket," etc.

After we came down that night from the hills, we kept on

riding. The sun was already paler, and it was as cold by day as the nights had been, beyond the hill fires.

Bumpy ground, boulders, and ragged pines. Ravens flew over. I didn't pay much attention. Being so careful, as I was, to keep my distance and not speak.

Argul rode always a little ahead of me.

We came to a village inside an untidy wood fence. I thought, *He's going to leave me here.*

He didn't. When I asked, "Is this where—?" he said, "I'm taking you on to the town."

"Thank you. Can we talk then?"

"I've said yes."

We stayed in the village overnight. There was a kind of big room, divided by a leather curtain. I slept on the "Women's Side" and thought he would be on the "Men's Side"—but he wouldn't even do that; he went off to sleep in some other house. (The houses had pointed roofs, and the people had pointed, fed-up faces. Cold. Oh yes, cold in every way, weather and heart.)

No sign of Jelly. That was good. (I have to confess I've felt anxious about him—was he all right? I am nuts.)

Wrote up some of diary. Such a habit, now. Do it even when I don't want to, like now.

Would it be any use asking him to read this diary—as opposed to the fake one *they* gave him? Venn did that and proved to himself I was all right. But Argul—this *new* Argul . . . I can't really ask him anything, suggest anything. If he even lets me speak when we reach this town, then he won't *hear* what I say.

I could be making it all up. That's what he still thinks.

How can he think this of me?

Was I really always so terminally silly and underhandedly filthy? If so, why did he ever like me?

I go over and over what I will say to him when I *am* permitted to speak.

Then I get so nervous.

Then I want to slap him.

I want to *bite* him, I'm so furious about this *INJUSTICE*.

And then—despair.

Why *should* he believe me? Would I, if I were him? If he had just left me, and I was told he'd gone to be with the one he really loved, and I read that too in his own handwriting. And then he swanned back months after, chirpy, and said, "All a mistake. Heigh-ho, I was kidnapped. But here I am now. Of course you want me back."

Yes. I'd have believed him.

Even if I hadn't—could I have let him go if there was a chance he might want me still? I'd have given it one more try.

Maybe I'd have been a fool, but there. He and I were meant to be together. He knew that before I did. The glasslike science-charm he wore around his neck, that Ustareth-Zeera left him, showed him that—I was the one.

And now I can't even say to him, Pass the salt.

I can't even touch his hand by accident—which nearly happened the other morning when we were picking through some fur jackets and mantles, in some other run-down village. Our hands almost brushed each other, and he shot his hand away, as if I would *burn*.

He bought me the jacket, though. And this mantle, lined

with thick white fur, and the long leather gloves. (Nothing for him. His warmer stuff must still be packed.)

"Thank you for the winter clothes, Argul."

"All right."

". . . I haven't any money—you do know?"

"I know you are useless, Claidi."

"But—"

"Leave it."

He won't take any responsibility for me. Won't even let me freeze. I have to be safe and sound so he can desert me in this town we're approaching.

Isn't he cold yet?

He's still just in everyday wear, and I'm already well into the jacket.

This last place we've stopped, where we arrived today, (always spending most of the time apart—weirdly like when I was with Nemian on our journey to the Tower) is built up through rocks and caves, like a honeycomb. Not a sweet one though. It's the most depressing dump. Dark and cold, lit by very smelly fat-candles. Everyone sneezing and moaning, arguing, miserable, nasty.

This hostel-house is for "Unwed Maidens." Argul must have been pleased.

I've been more or less alone all day. I've sat writing by the guttering light, and outside, through a crack in the stone, which has no glass, not even a shutter, the drizzly lemon sun crawls from right to left over the smoky sky.

The girl with the slop-pail—yes, no bathrooms, either— just came coughing by, wiping her nose on her long hair. (Unfortunately, they all speak my language.)

"Off up north? Off to Winter, are you?"

"That's right."

"Be cold up there."

"So I've heard."

"This is boiling hot compared to Winter. Going to Ice-Fair?"

Am I?

"I don't know."

"Mind ice don't give way and drop you in the river. Be a deada in seven seconds from the cold of the water." And at last, I heard someone happy here, for off she went in merry peals of laughter at this enchanting thought.

"Wouldn't catch *me* there," boasted she.

After she went, I mooched through the caves to the stables where the graffapin is being not-very-well looked after. Gave him some food and groomed him. Cried on his neck. Mopped him up and regroomed that bit. He put up with all this, singing to himself. No glimpse of Argul's horse.

Of course, maybe Argul's gone.

At least still no Jelly. *Molded* by the Wolf Tower.

We all have been, in an awful way.

Did he really have something to give me? What? A bullet from the rifle probably.

Tonight Argul and I ate together in a big cave-kitchen. What with everyone else sneezing and grumbling so loudly, kicking each other, and flicking greasy food about, we couldn't have said much. Which was good, as we didn't say much. He didn't eat either, now I think of it.

Coming out, I stood back to let him go ahead through the door, and he did the same for me, and for a fraction of an instant, through trying so hard *not* to touch, his arm flinched against mine. His felt like stone.

"How long to the town now?" I asked. Trying to sound adult, sensible.

"Tomorrow. The next day."

"So soon."

He was gone.

But he hasn't been eating. Now I think, I've only seen him play with food. Is he still so angry and unhappy that he can't eat? And does that mean there *is* a chance—because if he still feels all that, he must care?

We have reached a river, and a shambles called Ice-Walk.

Even the way I feel now, I have to try to describe this, because it is absolutely strange.

We came uphill, and then the land swept over. From high up where we were, you see—The North. There it is.

The North is divided off by the straightest line of water, this river, which looks as though someone drew it there with a ruler.

A wide river too, a mile or so across, but from up here one could see the further banks. They were marble white. With snow. Only this marble snow, then, stretching away and away, featureless, a desert of white.

And onto it, constantly, a shimmering mist of new whiteness coming down, as new snow nearly endlessly fell.

The sky the far side of the river is purple—as dark almost

as night. But halfway over the river it's mauve, fading back to grey-white on this side.

Halfway over the river, too, the ice starts to form. From the high ground it looked like great dulled silver plates. These fused together as they neared the other side. Wedged up through the ice were *crags* of ice, very tall; they must be tall as hills? And curiously shaped, like complicated buildings with balconies and archways, spires, turrets—

The crags are overall white too, but in places an amazing transparent peacock blue *gleams* out, or luminous green. Shafts of daylight seem trapped inside the ice-crags, shining as the sky doesn't. But all the time, the light shifts, changes, and the colors, too.

Little lights sparkle down on the ice as well. What could they be? Oh, it's this Fair the girl told me about.

He was already riding off along the track, toward the un-inviting mess I've since learned is called Ice-Walk Town. It lies along the near side of the river.

And so this is where he is going to allow me to speak to him, and then leave me forever.

"There's a Fair on the ice," he said.

"I know. Yes. Are you—"

No answer.

The unadorable town looked like lumps of bricks to me. Extra-dirty smokes rose, clotting the whitish rain-not-quite-ready-to-be-snow.

The inn-room was empty, but for us. Everyone was always out at the Fair on the ice, said the inn-woman.

A fire groaned away on the hearth, warming the chimney and cheering the room only with smoke.

"Argul, please can we find somewhere more private?"

No answer.

He had sat down on a bench against the wall, stretched out his long legs. His eyes were fixed on that other place he looks at, in order to avoid seeing me.

"All right then. I've waited," I said, "I've had enough. Can I tell you now what happened? Yes?"

No answer.

I went and sat across the sort-of-table from him. (It was a plank on three stones.)

"I'll take it silence means yes, then."

Trembling. Panic and anger.

But I couldn't go on with this any longer.

So, I spoke.

Thinking back, I think I was pretty clear in what I said. After all, I'd said it to him in my head so often, gone over and over it, in proper order, leaving nothing out yet not exaggerating too much, I thought, or wandering off the point. . . . No, I think I did it well, putting my case. Explaining all that had happened. Why I left, where I'd been, how I got back.

Some of it does sound—how could it not?—incredible.

How long did I talk? Too long? My throat was hoarse when I finished—but that could have been the fire-smoke. (Once the woman came in and plunked a jug of something to drink between us, and lurched out again. Neither he nor I touched it.)

In the end, I'd said everything I could. I had told the truth. I said, "And, as always, I love you." And then I sat there.

He hadn't moved. Didn't look at me. Didn't even become fidgety, didn't sigh or turn to me, swear, or even say, "Claidi—now I see I had it all wrong—" None of that.

And now, too, he did nothing either, and the minutes stretched, became centuries.

I could hear a clock ticking over the fire. It didn't really tell the time, having only the minute hand left, but that went around and around.

Outside the window, was it darker?

"Are you going to say anything, Argul?"

He wasn't.

He just sat there.

The fire lit his eyes and gilded his hair.

"Argul?"

I put out my hand and set it on his arm. He didn't move. His arm felt like steel. He didn't even trouble to shake me off.

I removed my hand from his arm and rose.

Humiliating tears were on my face.

"Then Argul, you can go and put out your light—go and *fry*. If you're so stupid—so damned stupid—then what's the use?" My voice was shrill, then too deep. "That's it. You're an okk, blind and an okk. Where *I* went wrong was thinking you were all right."

And I raised the jug of whatever it was, and I slung the contents all over him. And then I ran.

I don't remember where I ran, saw nothing. The town might have been invisible, and the people didn't exist. I was all alone. I never even felt the cold.

◆ ◆ ◆

It was getting on to evening when I came back out of the nowhere I'd run off into.

I managed to find my way here to the inn. Had to, because my stuff is here. No doubt I should have been surprised no one had stolen it, but he must have paid, because my bag was up in a room on the second wonky floor.

Wind gusts blow, and the room swings one way, then another. It's like being on the sea-ship again, the ship he doesn't believe I ever *was* on.

He wasn't here when I got back. I knew he wouldn't be. Now I hurt so much I can't feel it, just numb.

Impossible. I shall never see Argul again.

The most stupid thing of all, I keep thinking how I threw the rotten beer, or whatever it was, over his hair and clothes. He *deserved* it. But I feel so bad about it, even now. His lovely hair, the cloak that wasn't warm enough. It's making me cry.

WINTER RAVEN

When someone knocked on the door of the seasick room, I ran to open it. I knew it wouldn't be Argul. But even so—

Flung open door.

Door hit wall and nearly fell off.

Outside—

As I had known, *not* Argul.

Face striped with tears, I drew the dagger from my belt. *"What do you want?"*

She just stood there.

Cool, she asked, "A little politeness?"

"Prance off."

"My," she said. "I've dropped by at a bad time, I can see."

I hated her at once. And that gave me back some energy, if not much sense.

"Look, if you want the bathroom, it's along the hall."

"Do I seem to need a bathroom?"

"Then *what?*"

"You," she said. "I'm calling on *you*. You're not a *bathroom*, are you? You do look rather *damp*."

Sarcastic horror.

"This is sharp," I said, of the dagger.

"So," said she, "am I."

She is.

Whatever I think of her, she is, she is.

Let me describe her, as I saw her there.

A young woman, my age, I thought, about my height, too, really, though she seemed taller.

She had very white skin, but a sort of *dark* whiteness. Eyes ink-black. Her very thick silky hair was chopped short just under her ears, and so black it looked like liquid. Strings of white beads looped in this hair, some ending in small gold disks. She had a necklace of heavier gold disks, set with round, polished pieces of amber. Her longish belted coat was black. Her boots were dyed strawberry red and had *silver bells* on them.

The two most astonishing things were (1) her cloak—a great swagger of a cloak that seemed sewn, on the outer side, with hundreds of black, black feathers, and (2) her good looks. She is beautiful. That's the only word.

Now she took a turn on the narrow landing in front of me. Showing herself off? Letting me know what I had to deal with? (She sounded, from all the jewelry, bells, beads, like a Hulta horse.)

"Coming down, then?" she said. "Claidi?"

"You know my name."

"I do."

"How?"

"We'll come to that later."

"No, you'll tell me now."

"Wrong."

Fortunately I didn't try to attack her. Instinctively I knew she would be able to disarm me and probably snap my wrist at the same time. Which I now think is definitely true. She's been trained to fight?

But I said, "Don't tell me, you're from the Wolf Tower too?"

"*Me?*" She gave a snarl of laughter. "Most people, I'd make them sorry they said that. But you—well, you've been having a funny time of it, haven't you, lately? What with unkind old Argul and all."

I swallowed. Then I slammed the door in her face.

Of course she flung it wide open again, and this time it did come off its hinges.

She strode into the room.

"Look, Claidi, name for name. How's that? I am called," she paused, understandably dramatic, "Winter Raven."

"That's quaint."

"*Thank* you. I think it's a good name. Meanwhile," she said, "my men are downstairs. And we have a friend of yours, all tied up."

"Argul—"

"Come off it. That man called Jelly."

"You have Je—"

"Jelly. Tied up in a bow."

In a kind of trance I picked up my bag—I was still wearing my coat—and followed her down the earthquake-y stairs.

It was true.

The first thing I saw, in the inn's mostly empty main room, was Jelly, curled into a really uncomfortable position, his knees up to his chin, and his hands behind his back, and all of him ringed by thick ropes.

He could just turn his head, which he did, and gave me his same old crease of smile. Despite the swollen bruise of Argul's punch, and how he was now placed, Jelly looked as he always had—awful. But unbothered.

There were also six men standing around the hearth, drinking from mugs. They wore black, like the girl, but on the back of each cloak had been outlined in gold the shape of a bird with curved beak and outspread wings. Ravens?

Winter Raven. *Raven.* Something crackled through my mind.

"This is Jelly, right?" asked Winter Raven, of me.

"Yes."

"We were pretty sure, but he wouldn't say. Despite what Ngarbo promised to do to him—" an approving nod at one of the six around the fireplace. "We don't usually cross to this side of the river," she added. "But under the circumstances we've had to. So. Your graff's ready outside. Shall we go?"

"Wait."

"*What?*" Impatient, she waited.

"*Who are you?*"

"You don't know? Thought you read about the Towers and all that junk, when you were at the Rise."

I said, "Raven Tower."

"Hey! *Claidi!* Wow."

"The Raven Tower was destroyed in the ancient wars between the Towers, in the City. That is what I read. Pig Tower and Tiger Tower and Wolf Tower survived. Raven Tower didn't."

"As you see."

The inn-woman came in right then, and Winter Raven strode over to her and handed her a great wodge of those bluey-green money notes. The woman stood speechless with glee, and somehow everyone else, including me, walked out, with tied-up Jelly carried along in the middle.

There was a boat to take us the first mile over the river, to where the ice starts.

Outside the inn, Winter's "men" had loaded Jelly in a sort of box on runners and attached it to his own horse, which also had a big bundle strapped on its back. That seemed rather unfair on the horse. As for Jelly, he was then dragged through the streets of Ice-Walk. People pointed at him in the box and made fun. No one tried to intervene.

I had already assumed I was a prisoner, as he was, though not tied up.

The others walked. I led Graff. As usual, he sang away to himself, snuffling peacefully. At one point *she* turned to me and said, "Don't you just love them, graffs; they're so easygoing."

"Divine."

She flashed me a look of scorn. "You know," she said, "when I think about it, I could really *kill* you."

"I thought you were probably going to anyway," I sulkily rejoined.

The boat waited by the quay. We got on, with Graff, and the horse pulling Jelly.

The boat was a sort of ferry. Lots of other passengers.

She walked off through the crowd and left me, obviously thinking I wouldn't simply jump off into the freezing water—where, according to that cave-girl, I'd be a "deada" in seven seconds. Perhaps I should jump? I couldn't face it. Oddly, I now found myself standing next to Jelly in his box.

As we were poled over the black varnished water, in under the canopy of purple sky, Jelly spoke.

"They've strung you along since Panther's Halt. Did you know?"

I didn't reply.

"Mmn," said Jelly. "I should have given you what I had for you, before. Can't reach it now."

My face was so cold it was best not to try to move my lips.

Jelly said, thoughtfully, "You don't know, do you? Shall I put you out of your misery? I must admit, it even had me—well, puzzled—until I came right up to you, on that hill."

Are my lashes freezing? Concentrate on lashes freezing.

"Argul," said Jelly, regretfully, "*wasn't* Argul."

"Oh, who *was* he then?" I screeched, scattering all the ice off my face.

"No one. You should have figured it out. Didn't you have

[95]

experience with those sorts of things? At Peshamba. Later at the Rise, in the jungle."

Now all of me seemed scattered. I fell apart.

I found myself leaning over him, gripping him by the collar. The bruise on his chin had gotten worse. Now he was all bruise. *"What?"*

"A mechanical doll," said Jelly. "Like the completely realistic Ustareth-doll which Ustareth left for Venn."

"* * * ?? !! . . . ?"

"Yes, madam. The ones who can make them, can make them *most* convincing. Have you forgotten—even Venn was fooled by the one he thought was his own mother? These dolls can even keep up a conversation, up to a point, providing it isn't too complicated. They can react and say the right things. And they can learn whole paragraphs to spout at you. Why do you think it kept telling you not to get close or touch it? It hadn't any warmth. Made of metal with padding over, and stuff that looks like skin. If you'd only rushed up and kissed it—" he shook his head.

I let go his collar.

He said, "See this bruise it gave me? I don't usually get done over like that. But it moved faster than a real man could. And, well, a steel fist. Lucky I did manage to dodge a bit, or it could have been worse. It was trained to do that, too—thump almost anyone who got in the way. It was your guide and guard."

Did I trust Jelly? *Jelly*—Believe him—?

Yes, oh yes.

"Why?" I asked. I added pathetically, "Why, Jelly?"

"To get you along here. It was meant to get you all the way over the river, judging from what this lot have been saying, all the way to a town on the other side. Not just to Ice-Walk. The cold, no doubt, affected its mechanisms. It broke down. So this Raven crowd who've been watching it—and you—had to come over instead and fetch you."

"How—watching me?"

"Spies. Even some way through the doll . . . until it stopped working."

That scene, which I would never—never will—forget. The way he sat across the inn table and never spoke. And even when I threw the beer over him—had he stirred? No. I'd thought it was his utter disgust at me, his self-control. But it had been because he was a *doll.* He hadn't been *Argul* at all—

"Jelly—"

"Mmmmm."

"Jelly—"

"—"

"They can *make* things like that? I thought only Ustareth could do that. I mean, that *real.*"

"Seems not. See that bundle on my horse? That's where it is now."

"—the doll."

"The doll."

I stared at the horse. Then back at him.

"Why do they want me so much?"

"I have a suspicion."

"Will you share it?"

Who is my true enemy—this Wolf Tower man, or *her*, Winter Raven, and *hers*. All of them, no doubt.

But Argul. It wasn't Argul—who hated me and wouldn't hear me. Not him. Not.

"This is getting a bit chatty, isn't it?"

Ngarbo, the black Raven, was standing over us, smiling crushingly.

Jelly's mouth closed up like something sewn together. He wouldn't speak in front of them.

He's brave, though he's horrible.

And Ngarbo may be handsome, but he's one of *her* people. None of them are worth anything. Even *she* isn't.

Why does she say she wants to kill me? What have *I* done to her?

The nose of the ferryboat grated into the ice.

More madness. She and I went off across the solid ice, to see the Ice-Fair (her idea, of course), and like friends, arm-in-arm, because she *took* my arm. Ngarbo, knives and rifle, swaggered behind.

"I ought to stop hating you, Claidi," she said.

"Please do. Then can I go?"

"Ha ha."

Would *not* ask her why she hates me. The Wolf Tower? My run-in with the Tower Law—how could it be that? I *destroyed* the Law—or tried to. Do these Ravens *like* the Law? They seem not to like the Wolf Tower itself.

The fair idled around the ice-crags which gleamed. They're called icebergs (she said). They never melt entirely, but sometimes a crack thunderingly appears. Slabs of ice that weigh a ton crash off and thump onto the people below. All good sport, it seems.

Torches burn on the poles, and braziers stand around *flaming* on the ice. It's so thick, only the slightest moisture forms around these.

Skaters, like at Peshamba, sailed by.

Winter Raven bought some hot roasted nuts in a cloth. She offered one to me. "No thanks."

What does she think I am?

Stalls on the ice sell everything. Marvelous colors. Another time, it might have been very fascinating . . . the silks and furs, the books with gold lettering on their covers, some in letters that look like curls or other strange shapes. The different foods—I'm hungry but will *not* say so. The jugglers and other performers. A bears' dinner party—I think they were bears, very big and well-groomed and hairy. A man sawing—I almost yelled—a girl in two pieces—in *half* they called it. How? As each "half" emerged from behind the screen, the girl had become *two* identical girls.

None of this was like the dreary shore with the town of Ice-Walk.

My life, too, has been cut in two pieces, and changed. Despite all misgiving and fright, I was almost happy. It wasn't, wasn't Argul.

But then . . . where is he? While I am here, *captured* again.

"Oh, look," said Winter R, sounding like an excited kid, "a fortune-telling bird!"

Up we skidded over the ice, bell-tinkling from her boots.

I looked at her in the torchlight. One minute she was like some haughty commander. Then like a child of five—

The bird sat on its perch. It was large, with sunset feathers and a long straight bill.

Winter Raven held out a coin. But the man seemed to know who she was and waved the coin aside. "Honor, lady. Good health to your Tower!"

The bird shuffled along its perch, jumped down, and landed in a big dish of sand. There it walked about, then dived its beak in, and came up with something, which it presented to WR.

Grinning—she even looks beautiful when she grins—she unwrapped the sparkly paper.

She read out, *very* seriously, *"Today is a day for making new friends."*

Oh yeah?

The man was bending over the bird's claw marks in the sand, as it hopped back to its perch.

"But also, lady, beware. An enemy—" He looked genuinely uneasy for her.

"Oh, that," she said. She gazed at me. "Is that you, Claidissa?"

I turned away, and the bird whistled mockingly.

"Your men have pulled Jelly out of the box," I said flatly. "They're rolling him along the ice." This made me feel very uncomfortable. I added, "I don't think they'd have got the better of him in the first place, if he hadn't already been hit and knocked out and bruised." She only glanced. "Rolling him along? Hit and bruised? Good," she said. "Wolf Tower scum."

Then she dragged me sliding off.

✦ ✦ ✦

Her men did everything she told them to, even to loading Jelly back in the box again, but not until one of them had kicked him.

When this happened, I went over and slapped the man's face. He looked surprised and raised his fist—and *she* shouted, and he put the fist down.

"What's it to you?" said her man, who I'd heard her call Vilk, to me. "Fancy him, do you? Eh, grandpa, lady *fancies* you."

Jelly (who wasn't *that* old) looked rather ill, but blank. As if none of us were there. His skin, under this dusk-day sky, also seemed darker, sort of blue, and his scalp-stubble was growing through fast. His feet are so big. He's disgusting—but, well, what harm has he done me really? He may even have helped.

"I only thought," I said, "kicking him like that, you might have hurt your poor leg, Vilk."

"Come *on*," said she.

We walked through the rest of the Ice-Fair, as if it were invisible.

The further shore was steep. The Raven men helped the horse pull Jelly. She and I helped the graffapin. He kept sliding and sitting down. We had to be careful, though *Graff* didn't seem upset.

"The snow-road up there is better," she said. "He'll be all right on that, won't you, boy? What's his name?"

"Graff."

"That's what they're *all* called. Couldn't you even *name* him?"

This was beneath me. (He had *come* with that name.) I ignored it.

We arrived on the far shore. Now we were across the river, in the North. In the winter-white snowland.

Right then, the snow didn't fall, but the sky must be full of it, ceaselessly making it.

There was no landscape. It was a forever of white, which even in the gloom shone like the moon does.

But the road was there at once, and you couldn't miss it. Though nothing else stood out on the landscape, the entrance to the road did. It was marked by two enormous stone beasts. A hundred feet tall? They were shaped almost like square, four-legged tables, with long necks that rose and rose. White stones, splotched with a sort of pinkish stone in patches.

"Giraffes," she said to me. "The town's full of live ones. Long-haired, of course, for the cold. Your Graff is part giraffe. He's going to love it there. Cheer up, Claid. You'll like it too."

"You think so."

"I haven't been fair to you, have I? Mother'd go on at me."

I tried to picture Winter with a mother, going on, telling her off.

"She's a lady of the Raven Tower," I said.

"*The* lady of the Raven Tower."

"Right."

Winter looked at me long and hard.

"You really haven't worked it out, have you?"

"I'm very slow."

"That's fine," she said. "It's been good, paying you back."

"*Paying me back for what?*"

"But not fair," she infuriatingly went on, "no, I haven't been fair. Look, there are the zleys."

I looked where she pointed, and at the zleys. Four high-fronted vehicles, carved, painted rich reds and magentas, and gilded, strung with bells like her boots. They have runners, which glide over hard-packed snow, as if on a road. Each zley was drawn by a team of three cream-white panthers.

"She bred the panthers," said WR.

"Who?"

"My mother. She's really a genius. Bred the graffapins too."

"And she can also make extremely lifelike dolls, real enough to be taken for human beings—is that her as well, this genius?"

Offhand, "Oh, yes." As if she'd known even very slow Claidi would work it out in the end.

But this had begun to sound like Ustareth-Zeera. Yet I know she is dead. Who then, is *this* one, this Raven woman, who makes clockwork people—or however she does it?

"*Who* is your mother?"

"Thought you'd never ask. You'll *know* the name." Something crossed her face—anger, a jeer. Then, almost preparing me—pity. "My mother is Twilight Star."

As they were pulling the wrapped bundle off Jelly's horse and into one of the zleys, I walked over and lifted the cloth away. There he was. There *it* was. I'd told myself I must get a look at the doll, to make sure. I'd been dreading it rather. Now—I just looked.

Argul lay there. Only not Argul. Lifeless, solid metal, clockwork . . . It no longer even looked like him, somehow. Oh, when it had been with me, it had been made to seem to breathe, to blink, to *think*. But —how could I ever have thought, even for one second, this was *Argul?* You see what you expect. Get what you look for. I'd been thinking he would behave as Blurn had done. And they had made him behave exactly like that. But oh, again, *how* had I been fooled?

I tapped its chest. Hard, metal, un-human—

My legs nearly gave way.

It was Ngarbo, moving in as if to catch me when I swooned, who brought me around. I straightened up and glared.

"Why don't you undo that man, I mean Jelly. At least don't keep him all folded up like a sandwich. There are six of you after all. Or maybe you're still too scared of him?"

"What," said he, all charm, "the Wolf Tower bod? We've already loosed him. Can't have him getting uncomfy. Not yet, anyway."

They had undone the ropes. Even tucked him in the zley under a fur. But Vilk and Vilk's gun were Jelly's seat-mates.

The men took three zleys. Winter was driving this zley with me. She rapped her command into the dark air. Part of the snow leapt forward—the panthers. We were off.

CHYLOMBÁ

Shall I describe this room first, or the town? Or the zley ride? That might have been glorious, under other circumstances.

The icy, lemonade-y speed-wind, rushing spangle-sprays of snow, runners going *zzsrrrh*, and all the jingling bells.

Graff trotted fast behind, steady on the solid, frozen snow. The horse had no trouble either, particularly without Jelly or the doll-thing. Sometimes the Raven men sang or shouted. And Winter Raven joined in the song. (Her voice, of course, is very good.)

Only Jelly and I kept quiet. A lot to think about, Jelly and me. I *wish* I didn't feel so much abrupt kinship with him. He too is my enemy. But we are now both prisoners of the Raven Tower. Even if—even if Twilight Star is my mother.

Everything has seemed to link to Twilight, in a way. Or does so now. If—I am her daughter, then Winter is my—sister. We're not much alike. I've never been sure that what Jizania said about my parents was true. Am I now really going to learn? If so—*when?*

The town is called Chylomba.

It's encircled by walls, which, where the snow is melted off them, burn with color. The whole town does that. Even when the sky fills with night—which anyway eerily reflects back the snow and the lamps, and goes a kind of metallic tangerine. Lamps light everywhere. The streets, the town hills, and the builidngs. But these lamps are also colored, like cats' eyes or gems.

Snow never stays anywhere for long, except on the roads, where gangs come by to pack it down hard. Even if snow covers the buildings, it melts off soon, due to a form of under-brick heating. (So the old servant says.)

Chylomba looks, from up here, like a toy. Lots of colored towers, and also all these little terraced hills, on which little pavilions or small towerlets perch, and they are the most colorful of all. From my high windows, I can see several of these hills. One is mauve. By which I mean every terrace, and its crowning pavilion too, is a mauve shade. Then there is one that is all a sparkly crimson. Over there, facing the sunrise, if ever the sun comes out, one hill blazes gold—I do mean gold, not yellow. No, the primrose yellow hill is over *there,* more southward. . . .

All this, with the snowed-white straight streets and squares cutting through, makes the town, more than a toy, look like a board game.

I don't like that. For if the buildings and hills, streets and squares of Chylomba are the board of a game whose game? And *who* are the game-pieces, the counters, or whatever?

High up, birds wheel. Actual ravens, I suppose. But if so, their way of flying is odd, and also they look too big.

This *room* is very big. Always warm.

Everything velvets and assorted furs. So many furs I was relieved when the old servant told me most of these are false fur, man-made, as they do it at Peshamba.

The ceiling is painted like a summer sky. With, naturally, a flock of ravens painted in.

The day sky is seldom blue outside, over Chylomba. Now and then a break comes in the cloud. It never lasts. Frequently snow falls, thin, like a mist. Once, muffle-thick.

"Is there ever a thaw?"

"No," said the kind old servant. "*This* is a warm season."

I watch the buildings go white, then all the color melt back through.

Always, day and night, lots of coming and going. Along the streets, zleys rush, drawn by panther-teams. Riders trot along, some on horses, or on graffs.

The *giraffes* pass too, like stately towers on table legs. They have long, grey-white fur, mottled almost with the markings of leopards. No one rides them; they just seem to roam at will. Once I did see one relight a lamp that had gone out, using a sort of wand lifted in its mouth. A giraffe-accompanying crowd applauded and then fed it things.

I've been here, in the Guest House, since yesterday. Nothing has happened, except down in the streets.

At first it was nice to wallow in a hot bath, to find clean, glamorous clothes that fit, hung ready in a cupboard.

The old man, or a girl, take my requests for food and bring me anything I ask for, even though I've tried to ask for things they *couldn't* bring.

"Where do you grow *pineapples* in this snow?"

"The hothouses," said the kind old man.

I'd heard his name. It had sounded familiar. Perhaps it's like the name of someone I've known. What was it? I'm afraid I've forgotten.

I'm not quite a prisoner. I can leave my room and trail about through the Guest House (now and then meeting other "guests," who all seem either in a Chylomba-type hurry, or as dazed as I feel).

Am I a "guest"? The town is also, they say, free to me. I can go where I want, I've been told. (Graff is ready in the stable. Or they can provide a zley.)

Yesterday, on arrival, I asked about the two relevant matters, but only once. I asked Ngarbo.

"Where are you taking that man Jelly?"

"To be questioned."

"Oh." I'd shaken inside, wished I hadn't asked. "Questioning" may mean all sorts of cruelties. I did say, "I know he's from the Wolf Tower, but I don't think he knows much, really." Though even I didn't believe that.

Loftily, Ngarbo said, "Leave it to us, lady." Patronizing twerp.

We were by then standing on the steps of the Guest House, in the new-falling snow. Despite everything, I'd dozed off in the zley and woken up coming in at the town gate, guarded by guards in black and gold, under a weird snow-light sky. Next moment it seemed the zley stopped. She, Winter Raven, sprang down and was gone, tossing the panther-reins to a groom in passing. Not a word to me. She'd probably said enough.

In the lamplit snow and muddle of moving figures, I lost her at once.

Stuck-up Ngarbo then took charge of me. He took me to the Guest House. We were on the steps when I asked my two questions. (Which I'd have asked WR if she had stayed.)

The second was, "When am I to meet Twilight Star?"

As I might have guessed, he just looked at me and raised his eyebrows.

"Are you meeting Lady Twilight?" he drawled.

"*Yes.*" What other outcome could I expect? "So, tonight?" I said. "Tomorrow?"

But Ngarbo only said, "Search me."

I hadn't been able to see what happened with Jelly, if they mistreated him again while dragging him off somewhere.

Before I could think of anything else to demand (uselessly) of Ngarbo, an old man undid the Guest House door.

"Tower guest," said slap-deserving Ngarbo. He didn't give the servant my name. He told me the servant's name—no wonder I don't remember.

I don't want to ask the servant what he's called.

I've been a servant myself—I was the lowest sort, a maid. And it seems so ignorantly insulting, immediately to have forgotten his name.

This is the END!!! (Which I thought had already happened.) (Several times.)

I stamped back to this posh room and *threw* things and

shouted, just like some spoiled brat—Jade Leaf at the House, for example—

Now I'm sitting here, and in a minute one of them is going to come and knock, ever so courteous and flirty, on the door. "Oh, Claidissa, are you ready yet?"

And I have to go out with them, pretend to be—well, not pleased—but pleased-in-spite-of-myself. In order to find out what is going on. If that's even possible. Which I doubt.

Because this is all a game. All of it. That becomes more and more obvious. I am angry. So very—

Sorry! I apologize. I mean, I know you're perhaps used to me by now, but you don't know, do you, what has happened?

Right, I'll tell you.

This being my second day here, and nothing having changed, no one arrived to speak to me or summon me—I thought I'd have to make a move.

I keep thinking how I was stuck at the Rise. I have a kind of sore place in my mind where I recall Dagger saying to me that night I found the Hulta, "It doesn't sound like you—didn't you try to get away or *do* anything?"

It's as if I have to keep on an extra amount now, to shut up her voice in my head. I keep wondering if I've gone soft, or sloppy. I mean, should I have tried to run away yesterday?—or at least tried to get to see this woman Twilight, who may—or may not—be my—

My mother.

Anyway.

Today was getting on for sunset. The purple cloud had cleared a lot westward, and a flaming band of apricot sky appeared, where the sun was thinking of sinking.

I went out through the very straight corridors here, which snap one into another, all alike, with endless doors and silk hangings. Then down a straight wide stair.

Below was a long room I hadn't seen before. Its walls were hung with what looked like carpet. Two posts at the stair's bottom had ebony ravens carved on them. There were carvings of ravens everywhere else too, and even painted portraits of ravens. Flying, sitting, doing clever things—like holding little flags in one claw, or, in one case, riding on a large rabbit. Under these pictures were brass plates. They said things like, "Ninth Raven Imperial: Jorthrust." "Twenty-second Arch Raven: Squawky." "Lady Maysel's Raven: Parrotine Inkblot."

Bemused, I was reading these, when I heard a door open behind me.

I turned around quickly. It was a man. He and I let out a yell.

Then, he yelled over his shoulder. "Hey, man. Come and see what's in here!"

Then the other one stepped through.

Framed in carpet and ravens, there they stood, gazing at me. Hrald and Yazkool. My first abductors.

"What are you doing here?" I tried not to scream at them.

"Might say the same," droned Yazkool.

They looked sick makingly elegant. Spotless finery, all in icy whites. Even their hair—Hrald's tinted greenish pale and Yazkool's palest blue. I just knew they had matched themselves in color to the Cold North. A fashion in Chylomba?

I'd last seen them at the Rise. Then they'd vanished suddenly from a terrace, leaving their breakfast, broken plates, and toppled chairs. And later Venn told me how he thought they must have been grabbed by some sort of gigantic preying swooping bird. Venn's favorite servant, Heepo, had vanished like that too, he said, when Venn was about seven. One second there—then a flick of shadow, and gone.

But H and Y are so unreasonable. It had always been hopeless trying to find out anything at all useful from them.

So now I tried to look casual. Thought I succeeded.

"Well, it's fascinating to meet you both again."

"Likewise," said Hrald.

"Speak for yourself," said Yaz.

"Ssh," said Hrald loudly, "look how hard she's trying to be cool."

"Bird that carried you off not eat you then?" I asked. "Didn't think you were tasty enough? Might give its kids food poisoning?"

"Bird!" They both howled. They both went into fits of laughter, holding each other up. "Bird—*bird*—she thinks it was a bird—well, she *would* think that—wouldn't *you* have thought that, Yaz?"

"Oh yes, Hrald, I would—"

They fell into chairs by the raven-carved hearth.

Don't say anything, just wait.

But they went on and on laughing.

Finally Hrald surfaced. He stood up again.

"How do you find it here, Claidissa? They treat their compulsory guests well, don't they? Every luxury. I've even taken up the mandolin again."

"I'm so glad," I said.

He waved me into a chair, wouldn't sit down again till I had, though Yaz sprawled there.

Hrald took out a tobacco beetle from a beetle-box. Yaz produced a long blue tobacco pipe. Clouds of fragrant smoke coiled around the ravens.

"Oh yes, no expense spared," said Hrald.

They rightly thought I too was a "compulsory guest."

"Have you seen the town?" asked Hrald.

He was always deadly keen on travel and sightseeing. I said, "Not yet."

"Let's go out then. They do a splendid meal at the Raven Tea-House. And there're the Winter Gardens—and all the Hills."

"Primrose Hill," put in Yaz, "Red Hill—"

"How can you resist?" said Hrald.

How could I?

So I said I'd go and put on my coat and gloves.

"Oh, and maybe not those clothes—a *dress?*" asked Hrald, not wanting to be publicly embarrassed by me.

I'd realized why they have, as I do, the run of the town. No one can escape here. Chylomba has those watcher things, those machines that watch—I've seen them on the upper parts of buildings. Also, the walls of Chylomba are high and the gates guarded. Outside, the snow.

Upstairs I changed. Sweetly put on a dress for them. Brushed my hair, powdered my face, and did my eyes.

Then I went mad and flung things at the wall—cushions, some crockery. The crockery didn't break. It wasn't even satisfying. (Though I'm glad in a way; it wasn't the cup and saucer's fault.)

Ah—there's the knock.

"Be right out!" I twinkle.

AN EVENING
WITH ENEMIES

The man with red hair pointed at the orchestra. Seven trumpeters stood up and played a fanfare. The vast roomful of people rose to their feet, clapping, cheering, raising glasses and cups. All those smiling, glad faces.

We, all three of us, looked around to see who had come in. It was us.

"Too kind—oh, well, too, too . . . No, no, really—"

Hrald and Yaz bowing and preening.

I was too startled to do anything much. *Why* was the whole of Raven Tea-House making such a fuss????

We were led by a smart servant woman up to a high platform at the Tea House's center.

Here we were placed at a table with red plush cloth and

flowers in a vase so tall they went up six feet taller than we did when seated.

"What are the flowers?" I confusedly asked.

"Orchids," replied the woman.

"They're good . . ."

"Some shall be sent at once to your room."

"No—er—it's all right—"

She'd gone.

Hrald and Yaz looked properly impressed.

"We've never had treatment like this before," said Hrald. "It must be because of you, Claidissa."

The fanfare was still ringing in my ears.

Everyone in the Tea-House had settled down, gone back to their food and drink and friends. But now and then, someone would catch my eye, raise a glass again. To me.

Me?

Why?

What did we eat?

H and Y had some roast thing, a hippotamus it looked like (hope it wasn't) from the size, as it rested by the table on a dish *longer* than the table. I had—what did I have? Tomatoes on toast, I think.

Yaz became very loving to me, in an untrustworthy way. Hrald seemed actually in awe, kept saying, "Shut up, Yaz. Can't you see she really is important here?" But Yaz only said, "Give us a kissy, Claidissy-wissy."

They drank a lot of wine.

Then the orchestra came up on the platform with us and played a song just for me. It was in some language I didn't understand, though everyone else seemed to. I was so self-conscious I poured tea in my glass of wine.

Then, to my utter disbelieving *horror,* everyone in the Tea-House started doing it. Tea into wine, or wine into tea. Servants were rushing everywhere with extra bottles and teapots.

"A new fashion," warbled Hrald. He did it, too.

Only Yaz wouldn't.

I began to prefer Yaz.

"Perhaps we could go on somewhere," I said, as they began to tire of the roast, and the chocolate thing they'd had after (which was nearly as big as the roast, or had been before they ate most of it.)

"Yes, up the Lavender Hill," said Yaz. "Romantic place. Might even be a moon tonight." He smiled grimly.

Hrald, the sightseer, said, "The terraces of Lavender Hill are laid with amethysts and planted with lavender trees."

"Or the Gold Hill," said Yaz, "pure gold hardened by silver. A *long hard drop to the ground.*"

Someone else was walking over.

What *now?*

"Oh, Ngarbo!" yodeled H and Y in happy voices, "Come and have some of this chocolate-cream giraffe." (It wasn't, was it?)

Ngarbo flung himself marvelously into a seat, which started to look more attractive itself, simply because he was in it. He wore his splendid Raven uniform, black and gold. His face, though, was rather spoiled by a nastily-split lip and half-closed right eye.

"Is it war?" said Yaz. "Has Ironel sent Wolf Troops to rescue us and take us back?"

"Why would she want you back?" asked Ngarbo. He shot a (half) look at me. Then back at Y and H. "There's been some trouble though."

"Nothing to do with us," said Hrald. "We try to be good."

"No, it's *her* friend, Jelly," said Ngarbo. He helped himself to wine, as a servant quickly carved him a great slice of the roast, with vegetables.

"Jelly isn't," I said, "any friend of—"

"Escaped," said Ngarbo. Then forked food into his damaged mouth with care.

I am of course mental.

When I heard him say Jelly had escaped, it was as if I lit up inside. *Jelly.* He is yukkily terrifying and evil. And from the Wolf Tower.

But the way they had treated him—

"Was this," I mildly asked, "before or *after* you, um, *questioned* him?"

"'Fore," said Ngarbo. "We were taking him to Raven Tower, and the umblosh" (some new rude word?) "suddenly got free of his bonds, thumped Vilk out cold, bashed Beaky on the nose—it's an easy target with Beaky—and smashed me, as you see. Then he was off and away. We fired," he added. "Missed."

"Oh *dear*," I said.

"Madam wasn't pleased," said Ngarbo, gloomy.

"That's the fair Lady Winter, is it?" asked Hrald.

"Yeah, she didn't like it. Nor the lady Princess Twilight."

At her name—Twilight's name—I got hiccups.

Oh, wonderful, Claidi. Up on a high platform in front of three hundred people, after a fanfare and so on, and hiccuping,

Surprising me, Ngarbo leaned over and slapped me on the back, which stopped it.

"He's one brave bod," said Ngarbo, "that Jelly. And clever. I'll give him that."

"Where is he now?" I wondered.

"Up in the mountains, no doubt," said Ngarbo. "We were on the mountain road when he got loose, going to the Tower. Search parties are still combing the snow."

"What does umblosh mean?"

Ngarbo thought. "Prisoner," he replied.

About twenty other people, complete strangers, went with us, H and Y and N and I, around Chylomba.

We went up Lavender Hill, where the lavender grows in warmed tubs among the amethysts. And also up Red Hill (rubies, garnets), Copper Hill (copper), and Primrose Hill— which is topazes and primroses. Are all these precious stones real? They look as if they are. In the end, you just get used to it, treading over slabs and pebbles that are jewels.

The Winter Gardens are at the top of Silver Hill (silver). Our twenty-four footsteps clanked and clanged on the steps.

By then the moon had risen in a half-clear sky.

The Gardens are partly heated and partly not. The snow lies on the ground, thick and white, and some of the trees are hung in snow like lacy blossoms. Other trees, evergreens, yew, eucalyptus, are cut in globes, arches, fountains, or animal shapes such as bears. And, big shock, ravens. There are holly trees loaded with scarlet berries. A heated fountain plays, a jut of liquid silver—like the Hill—but the edges of the pool are frozen, silver that has set.

There are ice statues, too, that look like tall people of milky glass.

The crowd that had followed us (me?) wandered about. Everyone pointed at the moon, which, like the sun, in the North isn't often seen. It too was an ice sculpture.

"So, it wasn't a giant bird that carried you off at the Rise, Yaz?" I asked.

"No, it was—" Yaz smiled, "a *raven.*"

"A monster raven?" I probed.

"No. Just a raven. Really two ravens. Another two got Hrald. At breakfast, you see. And then—up and away."

We were sitting in a warm arbor. Hrald and Ngarbo had gone off like old friends. But none of us are friends, are we? Enemies, old enemies.

Yaz seemed more relaxed. I let him put his arm about me and tried to get some sense from him.

"So—ravens carried you off, these two—four—and brought you both here."

"We stopped a couple of places on the way. But about right, Claidissa-kissa."

He kissed me, but I managed to move, and he kissed the side of the arbor instead.

"Oops," said Yaz, not really put out; well, it was quite a nice arbor.

"Are you the only ones?" I said.

"For you? Of course I'm the only one."

"Yes, Yaz. But I meant are you and Hrald the only ones to have been carried off—by *ravens*—and brought *here?*"

"Nah," said Yaz. "You know," he added, "*I* play the harp."

"Do you? How sensational. Could you have seen an old servant man who was also carried off? And were these ravens a little bit not usual? . . ." His head leaned over on mine. He had fallen asleep.

I eased away and left him lying on the arbor cushions.

Outside, a white-haired girl came up.

"Would you sign this?"

"What is it?"

"The hem of my dress. I'll keep it to honor."

"Honor what?"

"You!" she enthused.

"Er. Sorry, I don't think so."

Somehow I didn't dare ask *why* I was so important.

Ngarbo and Hrald were peering over into a silver tank full of colored fish. Then I saw they weren't fish, but butterflies—

"Are they in *water?*"

"No. It's a picture."

"But it moves."

"True," said Hrald.

"Hrald," I said, "tell me about kidnapping me, then double-crossing the Wolf Tower and taking me to the Rise."

"Oh shush," said Hrald. "I don't want to think about the Wolf Tower."

"You used to LOVE the Wolf Tower."

"I've developed."

Ngarbo said, "Lady Claidis, just a word." He drew me aside.

We stood under a black palm tree whose bark was encased in silver, and from whose fronds hung icicles. Somehow it was growing, it was strong. The moon sailed over and put on a cloak of cloud.

Moon in a cloud.

I thought of that song at Peshamba. I thought of Argul for a second that seemed to last a month.

Ngarbo said, "Tomorrow, she wants to see you at the Tower. We'll need to start early, it's a longish journey by road."

"Who?" I said.

"Lady Raven, Princess Twilight Star."

My head went around. I said, "All right. I'll be ready."

"The road's good. Would you prefer a zley, chariot, or carriage?"

"My graff."

"I'll see it's arranged."

He's much more respectful now. More friendly too. (These friendly *enemies*.)

Someone else came up for me to sign something, his cuff. I wouldn't.

Ngarbo grinned. "They'll get used to it."

"Ngarbo, why are they behaving like this?"

With the unclosed eye he looked me up and down. "You don't know."

"I always ask to be told things I already *know*."

"Better wait and have the lady tell you."

"*You* tell me."

"Better not."

She is my mother. It must be that. I'm the long-lost royalty, refound.

I don't know what I think of that. Not much. And yet—

"Actually, I'd like to go back to the Guest House."

"Sure," he said.

Ngarbo walked me down the terraces. We were silent. The sky was closing over like his eye that Jelly had battered.

Was Jelly out there in the winter waste? What chance did he have?

On the street, a servant bowed me into a zley, this one horse-drawn. Ngarbo nodded and walked off in another direction.

On the pretty buildings, the mechanical watchers turn, *watching.*

EXCITEMENT BY WINDOW

My room had been filled with orchids like rainbows, spotted, flounced, and frilled. The scent nearly knocked me out.

As I was carrying some into the corridor, the old servant man came up with some hot chocolate for me.

"I didn't ask for—"

"Help you sleep," he said.

"You are very kind."

"I like to be kind," he said quietly. He looked at me. He has such—a *face*. Not wise, or cunning, but not foolish, or even innocent. A face that has seen and known many things but keeps inside only the memories it likes. Like being kind, and liking to be?

I sipped the drink. "Thanks anyway," I said. "Really."

With the door shut, the room smelled like the inside of a perfume bottle. Despite the cold, I opened the largest window a crack.

Now I'm in the comfortable bed. The steady light will fade and go out when I lie down. Tomorrow I shall meet her. Twilight. And then maybe all this tangle can be sorted out.

I dreamed about Argul. He was galloping on a chestnut horse, then a black horse, then a white horse—over the snow, along the road toward Chylomba's gate.

I was up in the air, looking down. Wanting him to get here but unable to do a thing.

And somehow, though the ever-altering horse raced on and on, it never reached the town.

Awake now. But I must sleep. I need to be alert tomorrow.

Well, I couldn't sleep again, despite the hot chocolate. The orchids still in the room were giving me a headache. I started to think, were they somehow drugged by someone—anyone of my new, and old, unfriends, who might prefer me not to be very well tomorrow?

Just as I'd decided to get up and put them all outside the door, I heard this awful soft scrabbling sound.

It was exactly the type of sound that belongs in a nightmare—or a ghost story.

Whispery, scratchy—creeping near.

Was it in the room?

I sat up slowly, when I would much rather have crawled right down inside the bedcovers. The light came on.

Then I realized the grisly noise was *outside*.

Something was scratching its way over the roof or walls of the building. Probably nothing, only a—surprise, surprise—raven. A real one. Or some other creature, a pet got out of a window—

Then I recalled my own window, which I'd left ajar.

I had an immediate idea that something *not* a pet, but unusual and dangerous and possibly supernatural, was clawing its way up the wall, aiming for my room, and look, there was my now bright-lit, open window, all ready *to let it in*—

Would it be more sensible to sprint for the window and slam it shut?—or for the door, which looked much nearer—

I made the wrong decision, it goes without saying.

Leaping from the bed, I sprang downward, caught my foot in my nightgown, and plunged headfirst among the orchids. There was quite a row as vases spun in every direction—nothing breaking, only going *bang-boingg* as they rolled into other things. Since I was now lying on the carpet, the light again went out.

The thick rug, and even the orchids, had broken my fall, and I didn't have time to worry about a new bruise collection, because right then I heard the window swing wide.

I vaulted up and around—the light exploded back on—and I screamed at the top of my voice.

The *thing* in the window, now stepping through into my room, held up a shapeless wodge that might once have been a hand. Out of the shapeless *bulb* of head, a voice said sorrowfully, "Please shut up."

I started a second scream—which stopped in a croak.

"Yes," said the sorrowful ghost-monster. "Thank you."

". . . Jelly?"

He sighed.

My eyes were better used to the light now, and I could finally see that what was there was not a demon or ghost, but a tall man, his hands and face wrapped in bandages, leaving just slits for eyes and mouth—

"Jelly—what did they *do* to you—?"

"Never mind," he said, quite crisply now.

"They said they *missed* with the guns—"

"Yes, they *can't* shoot," he said. Smug?

Right then, perfect timing, someone thundered on my door.

"Jelly—hide—get under the bed. I'll get rid of them."

As he crawled from view, I lugged the covers across, then pelted to the door, trying to find excuses as I went for the din I'd made—sleepwalking? A *very* bad dream—

Outside stood two ladies in beribboned wrappers and hair-curlers.

"This is too much," said one.

"Far too much. Even if you are who you are."

"Who am I?" I blurted.

They blew down their noses like annoyed horses going *ptusk!*

"Sorry. I'm sorry."

"You had a tantrum earlier," they said, more or less as one. "Throwing things and screaming. We guest-prisoners do get upset. We understand. And that one was before dinner. But now it's long after midnight."

"Yes, I see. I should have thought. No tantrums after midnight."

"Do your screaming by day," said the more curled lady. "Perhaps you'd care to join us when *we* do it. Poppy," she nudged the other lady, "has even found some *breakable* plates. And she's an excellent screamer. My knack is tearing pillows with my teeth."

"Oh—excellent."

They were chummy now, smiling at the thought of the jolly plate-throwing, pillow-ripping Tantrum Party we were going to have.

"Nighty-night!"

We waved good-bye around the door. I shut it and went back to Jelly.

As he crawled out, I felt new alarm at his bandages.

"Are you all right?"

"Obviously not. However, let's get on."

I sat down, and he sat down on the next chair. He handed me several folded papers.

"What is this?"

"A letter."

Well, I could see that really. It was even sealed. White wax, with the shape of a bird in it.

"Who is it from?"

"Suddenly you can't read?"

"I can *read*. My own language, anyway."

"Then read it. It's in your—this—language."

"Whose seal is it in the wax? A bird—a raven?"

"Vulture."

Still I sat there.

Jelly said, sounding grumpy, "Before she married Khiur of the Wolf Tower, she was from the Vulture Tower. Ironel."

Somehow I often forget about the Vulture Tower.

Trying to forget about Ironel, perhaps.

He has brought me a long, long letter from Ironel. Venn's grandmother, and Nemian's. (Argul's, too.)

The woman who was Wolf's Paw, giver of the Law.

"You're sure this is for me?"

"Yes."

"Is it poisoned?"

"I hope not. It's been in my pocket for months."

"What does it say?"

"*Claidi*—" Exasperated, he had called me by the only name I think of as mine.

It made me act. I tore the letter open.

It's *very* long. I read it all, somehow, in silence. Then again.

After that I got up and walked up and down.

Then I read the letter again.

He remarked, "The more you read it, the more it will say the same things."

"Why didn't you give me this before?" I said.

He didn't say, *I've been trying for the past hour.*

"The time was never right. You were often spied on."

"Now it is?"

"Now it's the only time left I can."

"You know what it says?"

"Maybe."

"How *dare* you know! Did she tell you—did you read it—?"

I was being very unreasonable. "I'm being unreasonable. Would you like something? A cup of tea—food—?"

"Eating through this bandage will be rather messy, don't you think?"

He wasn't talking to me as he had. Probably we've gotten past all that. I'm past everything now.

I read the letter again.

My dear Claidissa, it began, *I hope this finds you well—*

Of all the—

I mean.

Rather than copy it all out here, I'll just put down the "facts" (?) as Ironel gives them to me, all in her handwriting, formal yet as curly as the hair of Poppy and her friend. And also decorated in phrases such as, "Your time among us, which was of such flowerlike interest to us both."

Flowerlike *interest*—I'd been tricked, lied to, imprisoned.

Like now.

The Wolf Tower had made me follow Nemian to their Tower. The Raven Tower has made me follow Argul—who wasn't Argul, but a doll—to theirs.

What Ironel says is this:

First she reminds me of her family tree, her marriage and the results, which are here as I copied them into my other book, but with the other information I've gained since.

Basically Ironel had two daughters.

One (Alabaster) married a prince of the Wolf Tower and had a son, who was Nemian.

Ironel's other daughter was, of course, Ustareth. Ustareth was married to a prince of the Vulture Tower. He had that foul name, Narsident. Their son is Venn—that is, Prince Venarion, born at the Rise.

After Ustareth left the Rise—and Venn—she called herself Zeera, met Argul's father—and their son, of course, is Argul.

Ironel tells me *all* this, including about Argul. So she knows Argul is her grandson too!

"He helped you to leave the City and the Wolf Tower," she says. "A valiant and practical young man. As I would expect, seeing he is my daughter's other son." *Typical.* Even Argul is only any good because he is related to *her.*

But then comes the rest.

According to Ironel, she is not the one who sent the balloons after me, to capture me and take me back to the City for punishment. (She just vaguely says that others in the Wolf Tower, more Lawfully minded and unkind than she, wanted that.) Ironel says that, when she found out what was planned, *she* hired Hrald and Yazkool, paid them to reabduct me. Then whisk me over to the Rise and to Venn, where I'd be safe.

Can this be true?

She did it—to protect me? Why? Oh, she gives a reason. I am, she says, Twilight's daughter. And Ustareth and Twilight, when at last they met, were dear friends. They had for so long admired each other for their individual rebellions against the

Tower Law, and the House Rules. After meeting, they thought up some scheme or plan. . . .

What plan? Ironel goes vague again. She grandly says it's to do with Family, and the Future.

But anyway, getting me locked in the City cellars for fifty years wouldn't be part of U and T's plan at *all*. So she, Ironel, had me rescued.

During the kidnap, I recall Hrald and Yaz being nasty about Ironel. I thought they were trying to see if the others would agree and help double-cross her. But now I think they were just trying to see how far the others would take her side.

Ironel says she has learned since (how?) that I've left the Rise, come back, and got myself involved in searching for Argul at a town called Halted Panther. (Am childishly glad she at least has the town's name wrong.) But obviously she sent the letter and Jelly after me there.

Then she says this.

"I fear, by traveling further north, you are going in quite the wrong direction. Argul, after leaving his people, has made his way back to our City. To the Wolf Tower. He came straight to me. If you value him, then you must add this extra gold to his crown. He came disguised, evaded all attention, misled my slaves, and found me alone. He then declared that he was only too aware the Wolf Tower must have taken you. Even the faked diary had not fooled him for an instant. He had simply pretended to believe in your faithlessness in order not to involve his people in the plot, and so keep them safe from us. (His people are these horse-riders—Hultarr, are they called? Ustareth was always irritatingly untalkative about them, with me.)

"Argul, then, came to me on his own. He said he would buy you back from us with Hultarr wealth, which I gather is considerable. Or we might have him in your place, if we let you free at once. I replied that now, surely, we had both you and he trapped in the Tower, our prisoners. He said we might *try* to take him prisoner, if we wished. He would enjoy the exercise of killing every one of us."

She sounds proud of him. It—the letter—sounds *real*. I can just hear him, wonderfully bluffing like that.

Then she adds, all casual, she knew by then he was Ustareth's son. Again how? Had Ustareth told her all those years ago—but when? (She says Ustareth mentioned the Hulta . . . ?) (Let's face it, the Towers seem always to know almost everything.)

Of course, being U's son, and more important, Ironel's grandson, he's matchless.

She is not going to have him harmed.

I want to believe all this. Believe that he believed in me.

Ironel continues that now Argul is living in the Wolf Tower with her (bet he *loves* that) and knows he is a prince.

If so, why didn't he send me his own letter, with hers?

Did she "forget" to put his letter in?

"The man by whom I send my letter," she says, "may also be trusted to give you word from Argul."

And why hadn't Argul come *with* Jelly—or *instead* of Jelly?

I look at what she says about that. It's too dangerous to allow Argul into the North. (After he got into the Wolf Tower??) Since I, that is me, have gone unwisely rushing off in the wrong direction, fooled by the rumor that Argul put about that he would be going that way. (Which he did to protect the

Hulta, throw the Wolf Tower off his track.) But it seems the North is a Bad Idea.

"The North is Raven country. The Raven Tower is strong. Though they would be your friends, I am not sure of them in the case of my grandson."

So there we are. She wouldn't risk Argul, and he did what she said. And—the Raven Tower are my friends, are they? Is this because of Twilight?

I don't trust Ironel. I never have.

But Argul seems to have done.

Then there's Jelly. Can't trust Jelly, can I? Even with this message from Argul.

Disturbingly, she ends her letter with this:

"Claidissa, when you entered the Tower that day, boldly wearing before me Ustareth's own diamond ring, which of course my grandson, Argul, had given you, I knew it at once, even in its Hultar setting. So you see, Claidissa Star, I could have crushed you then, if I had wished to. But no, I let you break the Law in pieces. I let you escape. Think of that, when you are deciding whether or not I may now be believed."

Her name is signed all coils and flourishes.

She then adds this.

"*Argul*—such a barbaric name. I must advise him to choose another. Something more civilized."

That is so—*like* her. So—*true*.

SAYING GOOD-BYE

No time . . . The sky was getting lighter between the roofs of Chylomba. A couple of those huge birds I'm always seeing here were soaring over. What on earth were they? I stood glaring out.

"Go on then, Jelly. What message did Argul send me?"

Jelly made a slight noise, a cough or a grunt. But I didn't care anymore about his injuries.

"Said he hoped he would see you soon."

"Why didn't he come *with* you? *Is* he a prisoner of theirs— of the Wolf Tower's?"

"No," said Jelly.

I turned and glared at *him*. What a sight I like this, though, he doesn't seem so overwhelming. Even his feet seem to have shrunk. Slumping in his bandages, pathetic.

"If it were you, Jelly, would you trust Ironel?"

"Who else is there?"

"Quite."

I don't feel relieved or even very upset. Mostly furious.

"It's getting light. You'd better go," I said.

"Not going to hide me, then?"

"Look, Jelly, I don't know what's going to happen to *me* today. Ironel says the Raven Tower is my friend—because Twilight is there and she's my mother, presumably. But then there's Winter Raven, and she can't stand me. So you'll probably be better off getting out. Can you find a horse?"

"Mmmn," said Jelly.

He got up.

Stooping—he must be *badly* hurt?—he made me feel guilty after all.

"I'll go the way I came," he said.

"Oh, look—have some breakfast first, or a new bandage or something—"

He swung out of the window. *Is* he hurt? Could he move like that, so agile, if he were?

"So long, Claidi-baa!" he rasped, as he slid away down the roof, dislodging quite a lot of snow. Slipping over an edge—he just dropped into the dawn below. I suppose he's all right? Didn't hear a crash or anything.

Claidi-baa—how does he know to call me that? (Argul has talked to him.) How *dare* he call me that? (How dare Argul *tell* him—)

[135]

No time either for sleep.

I got ready, putting on another of the showy dresses from the cupboard. I walked up and down before the cupboard mirror. Am *I* a princess?

My bag was packed, and I put in the letter. Then, I took out the ring, the diamond. Ironel had known it, had she? I slid it onto my finger. It felt right, as it always had.

Full light arrived, as much as you get here on a normal day, when the old man knocked on my door.

He brought me tea and some hot bread. About the only things I could face.

"Thank you for all your kindness," I said. "It *has* helped."

He smiled.

I said, "Look, I'm sorry—that man, the Raven Guard who brought me to the Guest House. He said your name but I didn't catch it. What are you called?" Somehow, it didn't matter now, asking.

Nor did he look fed up. I'd known he wouldn't. He said, "I'm Hedee Poran."

"And—I'm Claidi."

"Yes, I know. Lady Claidis Star."

"Well . . . If I'm ever back this way, I'll drop in if I may."

He said, gently, "It would be a pleasure, madam."

"Claidi, please."

"Claidi, then."

He went out, and I was glad I'd asked his name. I might never see him again.

Five minutes after, a brisk Raven-Guard-knock announced

Ngarbo, and Vilk (unfortunately), looking brushed and polished. Even Ngarbo's swollen eye had opened up a lot.

"Are you ready, lady?"

We went downstairs. I said to Ngarbo, "That servant man is first-class. He must be ninety? Should he be working so hard at his age?"

"He likes the work; he's said so. Chose it. Caring for the guests. Some of them even call him by a nickname, they're so fond of him."

We went around a corridor-corner. Vilk said, "Old fool. Brought here by mistake is how I heard it."

Turning another corner, there was Poppy, her curlers under an ice-green butterfly of veil. She fluttered at N, but also at repulsive V. Then pattered up to embrace me.

"Buck up, lady," said Vilk, to her or me, "we haven't got all year."

Poppy was offended.

"I was only saying farewell, noble Raven."

"You've said it now. Three or four times you've said it."

Poppy said, "Now I'm upset. Oh, other noble Raven," looking piteously at Ngarbo, "would you be so kind as to tell Heepo I've been upset. He'll bring me a cordial."

"That's it, *Heepo*," said Vilk. "Old stick from that jungle place oversea."

"No, a *cordial*," bleated Poppy.

We were walking on, Ngarbo promising to tell Heepo on the way out, and I was breathing so fast I thought I'd burst.

"Heepo," I finally managed. "His name's Hedee Poran."

"Nickname. He was once servant to a prince, some kid,

couldn't or wouldn't say the whole name. It got shortened to Heepo."

Dear old Heepo—Venn had said that. For Heepo had been Venn's servant, carried off, as Hrald and Yaz had been—but years before them. Fifteen years or more.

"I must say good-bye to Heepo," I declared.

"Now, *she's* doing it," growled Vilk. "He's only a damned servant. Forget it. We're already late."

I stopped.

When they too stopped and looked at me, I thought of the incredible Old Lady at the House, Jizania, supposedly my gran, if Twilight is my mum. I put on an air of royalty as I had put on this dress.

I stared at Vilk.

"You know who I am, now."

"No—" he started.

"Be quiet," I said. "Twilight Star shall be told how you behave toward her favored guests."

Ngarbo was solemn. Too solemn?

Vilk looked nasty, but Vilk always looks nasty.

They took me to the room with all the raven carvings and paintings. They waited in the doorway, while one of the girls fetched Hedee Poran.

He made no comment, the old man, as I drew him aside under a very big picture of a raven balancing an orange, labeled, "Two-hundred-and-first Flight: Yak, Balancer of Oranges."

"I'm sorry, I don't want to shock you, Hedee—but you were with Venn—"

"Venn . . . ?"

"Prince Venarion Yllar Kaslem-Idoros."

His face paled, but he was steady as he said, "Yes, indeed."

"*I* was with him not long ago. He's always remembered you—always worried about how you were carried off—from a high balcony, wasn't it?"

"Ah," he said, "yes."

"Hedee—*how were you carried off?*"

"Lords of the Raven Tower," he began. He stopped. Ngarbo and Vilk were abruptly approaching. Powerful I might turn out to be, but right now there were limits.

"I apologize, lady, but—" Ngarbo said.

"Put a lid on it," said Vilk.

Heepo looked me deep in the eyes and said only three more words.

"*They can fly.*"

No one moved. In the silence, I heard myself say, swift and light, "Oh, Heepo, what a relief. I was so bothered they'd be stuck up there, on the roof."

A juicy pause.

"Eh?" said charming Vilk.

"Those poor ravens on the roof outside my window upstairs," I warbled. Inside I had turned to liquid ice. "I thought they were flightless and stuck. But Heepo says it's all right; he knows them and they *can* fly."

Heepo bowed.

"Mad old fool," grumbled Vilk. N and V looked at each other. N shrugged.

We walked through other corridors I didn't see, and out into the freezing appalling world of Chylomba and the Raven Tower, where—*they can fly.*

Oh yes, it all made an awful sense. How else had it been possible to take three grown men from the Rise, grasp them and lift them and spirit them away too fast for anyone to see where they had gone? Even Hrald and Yazkool laughing about ravens—birds—hysterically. They wouldn't have laughed much at the time.

And that odd remark of Ngarbo's about our journey today being longish, slow by *road*. What other way could we go? Over the hills? In the snow, that wouldn't be faster. So what other method was there? Only one. The air. I think I'd vaguely wondered if they had balloons.

Those figures I've seen in the sky—too big, always too big for birds—

Graff was waiting, groomed and saddled, on the street. There were to be ten outriders, seven on horses, and three on other graffs, these grey ones. Men with faces muffled against the cold, black furs and gold trim. All the horses and the graffs, including Graff, had been given plumes.

It *was* cold. So cold.

Somewhere a dog barked, coldly.

I am going to the Raven Tower. To these people who have captured me and are maybe going to tell me they are my friends, and I belong to them. And they may be lying. And they can fly.

THE TOWER

Raven Road goes over the Ups.

They call the country this because of the hills, up and down and up. The road cuts through sometimes, but often follows the curves of the hills, which are short and rounded, taking, each one, about ten minutes to ascend, five to go down.

Pines and firs like dark arrowheads stuck in the snow.

Beyond, above gradually the mountains appear from the thin, snowy mist. They seem at first to be adrift in the sky. Islands, cake-iced with white. They are hugely high.

I wonder if I Irald has made this journey, nudging Yaz, "Look at *that*—what a view!"

Don't think so, somehow. Not many "guests" get brought all the way to the Raven Tower.

Lucky Claidi.

She is there.

Venn would understand this, I think, the feeling I have now, iron cold on cold iron in my stomach. When we went to the house on the lake to see his mother, Ustareth. Only she was a doll.

But Twilight isn't a doll. Why am I so sure? *Argul* was a doll. (And the real Argul is in the Wolf Tower, being a prince with his grandma. How do I believe *that?*)

There is so little I can believe, I have let go. I'm just adrift, as the mountains seem to be, though not attached, as they are, to the earth, or to anything.

I've written this at a stop. They put up a silk tent, lit braziers, brought me a hot drink, and hothouse grapes. (Graff liked the grapes.)

"Only two or three more hours," says Ngarbo, encouraging.

"Oh, be gone in a blink," I say.

I don't dare say anything like, "We should have *flown* up, shouldn't we." I am afraid of the whole idea.

Most of the outriders sit huddled, broodingly, in twos or threes, or apart. I've brought them out when they had better things to do? Shame.

Anyhow, soon

I'll

see

my mother?

If you are still reading, hold a kind thought in your mind for me. Please. I'm alone, and I feel as small as anyone could, under those mountains, under this tumble of shadowy sky.

The Raven Tower rises suddenly out of the hills, among the lower spires of the mountains.

The Tower is enormous.

I remember the Wolf Tower as big and dark, but the Raven Tower is high as sky and black as coal.

The top of it hasn't got a statue, like the Wolf Tower. No, the top of the Raven Tower is itself shaped and carved like the head of a raven. Beaked, scored by feathers, glistening and black, with just a cap of snow. Seen from the Road, the head is turned. It seems to look sidelong at you, as a bird would. And where the eye would be, there *is* an eye—a great high window, fire red.

"Impressive, yes?" asks Ngarbo, riding at my side.

He is stuck-up over the Tower.

"Very nice."

"Oh, girl, come on."

Ngarbo was probably right. (?) But I'm not going to be friendly. Not now.

I leaned forward to pat Graff.

Graff was my *only* friend at that point. Dear old Graff, wuffling and burbling away to himself, singing in the silver air, with snowflakes melting on his lashes.

"You're just cold," said Ngarbo, making excuses for my loutishness in not praising the Tower. What did he expect!

But then, I didn't know what any of them really knew about me, or anything.

We rode on up the Road, up the Ups.

The snow was coming down more heavily now. The horses and graffs were trotting quickly.

An arch appeared, a hole in the hills, under the Raven. As we jounced nearer, I saw torches burning there. Then, I saw they weren't torches but more of the hard, still science-magical light.

How did they defend the Tower, out here in the snow-waste? There were no guards I could see.

As we got close, the dark arch undid itself. Doors swung back to reveal a tunnel. Very uninviting it looked. No one stood in the way. We rode through, and in.

"Who's that, on the end?" Ngarbo asked, craning back, as we clattered into the tunnel and the snow-Road changed to metal. The hard lights lit the way.

"Not an idea," said the other man, not Vilk, riding the other side of me. "He didn't sit with anyone at lunch. Looks like he's got in an argument now."

"Must be Eggblat," said Ngarbo, "He's always in a fight."

"No, Eggblat's off on his vacation."

I lost interest as they bickered over the last rider of the escort. What did I care?

Then there was a racket.

The metal-faced tunnel roared and rang, and even Graff was shaking his furry head.

Ngarbo and the other man went galloping back down the tunnel. From the lit dimness behind, men shouted and cursed, and then there was the sound of a shot.

Suddenly a rider, another Raven, I thought, muffled up and

black-cloaked, on a black horse, rushed past me and on up the tunnel.

All the others then also came plunging up the tunnel after him. I pulled on Graff's reins, and we just got to the tunnel-side out of the way in time.

Then we sat there.

We had been almost trampled by our escort, and left behind.

"This is lovely," I said to Graff, "isn't it."

I thought of turning around and batting off down the tunnel again, out of the doors—if they hadn't shut, or would open, off over the snowy Ups to somewhere or other. To freedom.

But right then Vilk rode back down the tunnel to me.

"Come on, it's safe now."

"Is it really."

"We got the rotten nerbish." *(What is that?)* "Well, he surrendered to us."

"Did he really."

"Thought we'd seen the last of *him*. Must be potty. What's he up to? Gets away—then comes *back* with us?"

"Who?" I asked.

I already knew.

"That Wolf Tower stinker *you* like. What's-his-name."

"Jelly," I answered.

It's carved up through a tall hill or small mountain, the Tower.

When you come out into what they called Hall One, everything is massive but rough-hewn, the inside of a vast towering cave. But it's warm, and not only from the two great fireplaces, alight at either end. There are hot-water pipes working. It's quite up-to-date.

In fact, of course, it's more than that.

I'd expected lifts, but no. Under the heavy banners, (showing ravens in gold on black, black on red, purple on gold) a stair piles up. It looked like metal.

"Hold onto the rail, please, lady," said one of my guards.

So I did. Just as well.

I gazed down queasily.

"The stair is moving?"

"Sure is."

This reminded me of the Rise, sections of building, stairways particularly, always diving about. But the moving stair of the RT isn't like that. It does it to be helpful.

And how had they made it move?

"That knob down there."

Why should I worry about this stair? They can *fly* upstairs if they want—or some of them undoubtedly can.

At the top, where the stair came to a standstill and we got off, was Hall Two.

Here I was asked to wait.

I sat in a chair, staring around at the soaring stone walls, not seeing much.

Most of the escort left me. (Lots of flaring cloaks. Cries of "By the Raven!" which I think I've heard them do before, but here it sounds sort of religious.) Ngarbo and Vilk had already gone, to deal with Jelly again, I imagined.

Jelly was certainly mad. But I hadn't room to think about him right now.

Then, through a high door, came drifting a maid of some very well-dressed sort. What I recall is that her hair had been dyed in stripes of black and lilac.

"Lady Raven will see you now, in the Raven Chamber."

I got up. How, I'm not sure, as I seemed to have no body.

I followed the maid across Hall Two, out of an arch and along some passages. Then there was an everyday stair, which we climbed. At the top was a door made out of complicated colored glass in patterns. It glimmered from some soft clear lights on the other side.

The maid opened the door, stood back.

I was to go in.

For a second, I couldn't move. Then I just walked through, the most ordinary thing to do. But this was the answer to my life I was walking into. The *reason* for my being alive, perhaps, and for much of what has happened to me. And I thought *wait*—but it was already too late for that. Because there were only two human figures in the Raven Chamber. I didn't need anyone to tell me who they were.

MY MOTHER

Two people—and about fifty ravens. The two women grew up like long-stemmed plants from a black grass that waddled and croaked, and now and then flapped up in the air and sailed over the room. Ravens perched in the raven-carved rafters, too. One swung back and forth, enjoying itself, on an ornamental lamp.

She had one on her shoulder. I mean, Winter Raven. She was dressed in a long, narrow white dress. The raven stood on her amber necklace, pecking the beads—silver today—in her hair.

The other woman was older.

How old was she? Old enough . . . to be my mother.

She had dark skin. Her hair was like honey, and her eyes like paler honey. (There was a little dusting of grey in her hair.) She was slightly heavy in build, graceful.

She wore a plain black velvet dress, and around her neck was a ring of gold from which hung a turquoise so finely cut and burnished, the dark of her skin showed through it.

She's beautiful.

She's Twilight Star.

"I am Twilight Star," she said. "My daughter you've met." She had an accent. What was it? Oh—I thought—it's the accent of the House, the Towers—which somehow I no longer have. I must have the Hulta accent now. I'd never noticed. "And you," she said, quietly, "I must call—Claidi."

"Thank you," I heard myself say, in my Hulta accent.

"Will you sit down?"

I sat.

It would be simple to detest her for being so *untense* and in control. But *I* didn't sound too bad. Was it costing her as much as it cost me, to keep calm?

Winter *wasn't* calm. She was snarling at me, sizzling. (My sister?)

A couple more maids had appeared. I was being offered a tray with glasses of this and that—including a glass of hot tea—which is what I took, mostly because the glass hadn't cracked from the heat. (As I took the glass, I saw Twilight's gaze flick over my hands. Was she looking at the diamond ring?)

"A long journey from the town, I'm afraid," said Twilight Star.

"Yes," I said.

"I hope you're not too tired to talk."

"No."

Winter had taken a glass of something bright blue, which

she drained in a gulp. As she turned and stalked away over the chamber, her shoulder-raven flared its wings.

"You don't mind birds, I hope?" asked polite Twilight.

"No." I drew in a breath. "What I mind—"

"Is being kept waiting for an answer?"

"Wouldn't you, madam?"

Couldn't call her anything else, could I?

She too had sat down by now, in a chair under a lamp. As the turquoise pendant swung, she touched it to make it still. She seemed one of those people whose every gesture counts.

A carved raven on a beam flew up. It was real.

Everything is like that. What seems fake is real, and what seems real—is a *lie*.

So, watch it, Claidi. Watch out.

"Why am I here?" I asked. "I mean, why did you try so hard to get me here? The Argul-doll and everything."

"Yes, we did try hard, didn't we? I'm sorry for that, the deception. But we wanted to see you. It was important."

"Why?"

"You saw how they treated you in Chylomba," she said.

"Which bit?"

"When they cheered and drank your health, and asked you to sign their clothes—and you—Claidi—being you, refused."

"Why would they *want* me to sign their clothes?"

"There's so much to tell you," she said.

"We'd better make a start then."

Suddenly she smiled. She said to me, "You are *exactly* the way everyone describes you."

"Oh, *smashing*. Everyone?"

"Mother," said Winter, from across the room, "you can see what she's like. Do you want *me* to tell her the facts?"

"No, thank you, dear."

"Then perhaps you ought to *do* it. You want that too, don't you, *Claid?* You want to know?"

I didn't even glance at her. I kept my eyes fixed on Twilight.

Twilight said, to Winter, "Darling, try to be patient with me. Or I'll have to ask you to wait outside."

"I *won't* go!"

"Then please . . ." Twilight folded her hands. "I'd prefer—Claidi—to tell you everything in some sort of order. So, I have to begin at the House in the desert waste."

"The House and Garden?" I asked. (*My* beginning.)

"Yes. But then, it begins before that even. When the Towers were at war, and the first Raven Tower was destroyed."

Her voice was smooth.

I felt I must sit and listen carefully.

Then, Winter Raven was laughing in harsh long shouts.

Twilight glanced at her.

Winter said, "Just look at her, mother. Like a baby waiting for a story. Hey, *Claidis-Claidissa*—how *old* are you, Claid? Three, or four? Thought you were my age, *Claid.*"

"My name," I said, "is not *Claid.* Or *Claidis.* Or *Claidissa.* My name is *Claidi.*"

Twilight's voice, no longer so smooth, like a knife's edge, cut through.

"No, I'm afraid it isn't."

I turned, staring at her.

"Oh, I am *sorry,*" she said. "But why go on pretending? Your name isn't any of those. Certainly not Claidis, nor the pet name, Claidissa. Those are the names of my daughter. She, the angry girl there, who calls herself Winter, is my only child. And Claidis—even Claidissa or Claidi—is not your name, never yours—but hers."

Now I know it all. I feel I have been *stuffed* with it like a cushion. Then sewn together around it. This knowledge. The Truth.

I sit here, stupid as a cushion. I can think of nothing, except what I've just been told.

All this way, for *this*.

I can't remember many of Twilight's actual words. Can't remember what Winter—no, what Claidi/s/ssa did. But I can remember the "story" Twilight told me. Let me write it down then. In case I ever forget and start to think I'm Claidi, ever again.

Long ago, in that ugly City on Wide River, the five Towers fought, made it up, quarreled and fought again. Pig Tower with Wolf Tower, Wolf Tower with Tiger Tower, and Vulture Tower and Raven Tower. In the end Wolf Tower won all the wars. Became Top Dog—Top Wolf.

Every Tower had taken a beating, lost men and women, lost land and property, been damaged. But the Raven Tower was totally destroyed. And most of the people left alive from the Raven Tower—they were made into slaves.

Worse than just having to be slaves in the City, plenty of them were sent to other places far away. There were lots of towns or settlements that had a link with the Towers. One of these was the House in the Garden. Years passed. I don't know how many—hundreds?

Jizania was from the Tiger Tower, but she married a prince of the House, Wasliwa Star. Finally they had a daughter, who they called Twilight.

Twilight grew up in the House, a princess, living a life of pleasures and riches. The one thing that got on her nerves was the endless Ritual, the Rules of the House. So she ignored them wherever she could. Especially she ignored the one about making friends with a slave.

Twilight's friend was the slave Fengrey Raven. He was descended from several generations of captives from the Raven Tower. He liked Twilight, too.

By the time they were twelve, they were inseparable. When they were sixteen, Twilight told the House that Fengrey was no longer a slave, but her steward. This caused an uproar. But Jizania was powerful, and so was Wasliwa, so Twilight got her way.

Fengrey and Twilight fell for each other. She said to me she thought they'd been in love since they were children. But when they were eighteen, she told the House they were going to marry.

The House refused.

Even Jizania couldn't change that one, and Wasliwa, by then, had died.

So Twilight and Fengrey lived as husband and wife, made no secret of it, in fact showed off, in front of all the House.

At first it was a scandal. No one would speak to them. Twilight laughed, didn't care. Then the House decided to pretend nothing unusual was happening after all, and made out Fengrey was only Twilight's steward still.

This went on for quite some time. Until Twilight found she was going to have a child.

Nobody in the House was allowed to have a child without permission. (!) *I* knew that. Slaves and servants who broke this rule were exiled at once to the Waste. Aristocrats were usually treated more sympathetically.

But Twilight's baby's father was a slave. Worse, a Raven slave.

The House exiled Twilight and Fengrey to the Waste.

When I was at the House, we—the servants—were told the Waste was hell-on-earth. Nothing and no one could survive in it. But in Twilight's time—and even in mine, perhaps—the royalty knew the waste wasn't all like that.

So Twilight and Fengrey got ready to leave.

Then the House inflicted the real punishment for their disobedience.

They were told they might not go until after Twilight's baby was born. Then, when they did go, they must leave the baby behind, to serve the House, a slave or servant, in Fengrey's place.

Probably for the first time in her life, Twilight had been out-thought, and was truly scared. As for Fengrey, he went crazy. *He* had had to grow up in this House of enemies. Now they would do it to his child!

Both Twilight and Fengrey were kept prisoner. Then Twilight's baby was born.

Twilight said her mother, Jizania, thought of the solution to the problem, and managed it.

At about the same time Twilight gave birth, so did one of the slave-women of the House.

Slaves counted for nothing. Only Fengrey ever had, because Twilight loved and valued him. So it was easy for Jizania to take the slave's newborn child away from her and give it to Twilight.

Jizania said, "Make out this slave baby is yours. Beg them to let you keep it. They'll force it from your arms. Meanwhile I will hide your real child, and see it comes to you in secret, and leaves the House with you. They can keep the slave-brat instead."

That's what Jizania said. That's what happened.

Twilight and Fengrey got away, with their own real daughter hidden in a basket of clothes and jewelry.

And the slave's child? Well, it was only a slave—the sort that wasn't fallen royalty from a Tower. Just a slave.

You could say it was even fortunate, because rather than being a slave, it was given to Princess Shimra, who had been Twilight's friend. And Shimra gave it to her own daughter, the unspeakable Jade Leaf, as a maid. And—that child, that slave-child—that was me.

My mother. That was my mother. My mother was an unknown slave.

Oh, I *asked* Twilight, Who *was* she? What was her *name?*

Twilight—I do remember her words on this—said, "I'm sorry. I don't know. She was a slave, you see."

Which means—she was *nothing.*

Nameless. My mother, the slave. Nothing.

I think back—how can I help it?—the times I saw slaves—dragging the princess about in chariots, being slapped, whipped, pushed around. Saw them sleeping in rooms like holes, in the House, in actual holes in the rotting tunnels under the Garden. Have I ever looked into my mother's face—and not known her? And did she know *me?*

I always said, I was no better than a slave there. I was right.

As for my father, well, obviously, absolutely no one could know who *he* had been.

Are they alive—or dead?

I've been asking that question since I was tiny and first heard my parents had been exiled, as I thought.

Twilight said to me, "Probably dead, by now. A slave—unless cared for—seldom has a long life."

After that, she was telling me how some of the other Raven Tower people had meanwhile gotten away and set up a new Tower in the North—or resettled an old Tower. I don't know. Who cares?

I'm a slave. I'm not interested in royalty.

But anyway, this Tower was here. And Twilight and Fengrey came here, and later, after Ustareth visited them, scientific wonders took place, and they lived happily ever after, Twilight and Fengrey Raven and their daughter, Claidis (nickname Claidissa—or Winter).

Then, there in the Raven Chamber, I heard Twilight and her daughter having this exchange.

Winter: "I think we might let Claid keep the name, don't you?"

Twilight: "Claidis is *your* name, Claidis."

Winter: "I don't *want* that name, I've told you, now she's been using it all these years. She's messed everything *else* up for me. At least let me keep the name that *I* gave me."

Twilight: "Winter is a false name, my dear. Your name is Claidis."

All this, as I sat there, broken open down the middle, stuffed with horror, and sewn up again.

I got to my feet in the end.

"I'd like to be alone," I said.

Oh my. Claidi-who-isn't, the slave's brat—I sounded like a royal woman. A queen.

I was—dismissing—*them*.

Twilight didn't react. She said, "Of course. But there is still a lot to tell you."

"I've heard enough."

"Another time, then. The girl will show you to your apartment."

But Winter stood there in my path.

"Aah, you feel sorry for yourself, don't you, *Claid?* You little *word-I-can't-even-think-how-to-spell.*"

"Get out," I said softly, "of my way."

The raven on her shoulder lifted its wings in alarm.

No, I'm no longer a slave.

Whatever the hell I am, I am *Me*.

Twilight said something to her as well. I didn't hear it. But I walked by, through the hopping, flapping ravens. As I reached the door, one of the low-flying ones gloriously relieved itself all over my shoes.

Wonder why that doesn't happen in there more often? Some other scientific trick, no doubt.

A striped servant brought me to this room.

✦ ✦ ✦

What shall I call myself now? I too don't know whether I want that name anymore. *Claidi.* It was hers, but I had to have it.

It's obvious to me Ironel never knew—still doesn't—that I wasn't Twilight's daughter. That promise Ironel had gotten under the Law from Jizania, to send Jizania's own grandchild to take Ironel's place as Law-Giver—how Jizania must have enjoyed that. Sending *me.* Slave-princess Claidi.

Someone brought me some dainty food, hours ago. It sits there, as I do.

Now they're knocking on the door again.

Let them.

This room is big. A big window shows the darkening mountains. Night's coming.

Still knocking on the door. I've called out, "Go away."

But now I think, it's some servant, some slave. My own kind. So I'm not going to be sullen and rude. I shall go and *ask* them to leave me alone. And if that causes trouble, make sure it falls on me, not them.

It wasn't a slave. It was her again. Twilight. She was alone.

"I understand this must be painful for you. But I have to finish what must be said."

As the dark comes, the lamps in here *fade up* into light. Nothing sudden. It's lovely. I hate it.

"And of course—*Claidi*—what can I say—you must keep your name."

"*Thank* you."

"It is your name, also. Forgive me. And forgive my daughter. She's very angry with you."

"Yes, terrible for her."

"Let me tell you everything. You may then understand."

"Madam," I said, "all I want is to get out of this tronking okk's grulp of a Tower."

Look at her. Oh, I'd have loved to have a mother like this. What is Fengrey like? Great, I expect. Plus the wonderful Jizania as granny.

No, I wouldn't want them. They too play with people, use us, move us about in this game the Towers like so much.

But she had sat down. As I stood, my back to her, looking from the window at the vastness of view, she's told me "Everything."

Here goes.

Ustareth, after she left the Rise, and had met Argul's father, made contact with Twilight, here. It was Ustareth who, with her magical (scientific) brilliance, altered the shoddy old Raven Tower to what it is now. Or rather, she gave Twilight the means to do it.

Twilight also made Chylomba, or had it made by machines. (And yes, the jewels on all those Hills are real ones, dug out of mountain mines, also by machines.)

Twilight speaks of Ustareth with loving regret. They didn't meet often. But they did think up this plan—a Dream, Twilight called it.

"The evil bullying of the Wolf Tower," said Twilight, "and of the Law. The Law, where it exists, is almost like a living thing. It rules over anyone who will allow it. Ustareth and I— we believed so strongly that no one should live that way."

And their idea to solve this?

"Ustareth said she and I were powerful. Not only in what we could do. In our hearts and minds. I don't mean cleverness. I mean strength of character, willpower—whatever names one gives it."

Ustareth had said that she and Twilight were superior in this way. They had fought the Law and won. But their children would be even better. "This can happen," Twilight assured me, earnestly.

So that meant Ustareth's son, Venarion (Venn)—even though his father wasn't so good. And her second favorite son, Argul, whose Hulta father Ustareth had loved.

"Ustareth's plan," said Twilight, "was that my daughter should, when grown up, marry one of her sons. Both boys were older than my Clai—" she had the grace to hesitate, "my own girl," she went on.

Twilight explained that Winter (what else can *I* call her?) grew up knowing that she would one day be married either to the amazing Argul, or to almost as amazing Venn.

"But then, in due course," said Twilight, "*you* met Argul. And then again, when Ironel sent you away to the Rise, you met Venarion."

By now I'd turned around from the window, I admit, and was goggling at her.

"First," said Twilight, gently, "you were using my daughter's name. Then Argul became yours. Then, so far as I can judge, Venarion, too. She's a proud, fine girl, who wanted to marry a man her equal. Are you surprised my daughter wants to kill you?"

"How do you know all this?" I said. "I mean Argul and me—Venn and me—" Of all the hundred questions, this one, *How do you know?* always seems to rear its head.

"My dear," said Twilight, "Ustareth's science left us all a great many means of knowing a very great deal."

"Ustareth," I said, "also left Argul a charm—a *scientific* charm—which would show him the woman who would be right for him."

"I know," said Twilight. "It was meant to show him, er, Claidi, that my *daughter* was *right* for him. Do you see? *My* daughter."

"*What?*"

"Am I only being a foolish mother, when I say I think he might have liked my daughter considerably, if he hadn't met you?"

"Are you telling me—" I stopped. "Are you saying the charm is *also* a LIE? That it somehow showed Argul *I* was the one for him because—only because—I'd ended up living your daughter's life—and with my—that—name—Claidi—Claidis—*Is that it?*"

"It isn't so simple."

"Nothing is. Answer me!"

"In a way."

I dropped in a chair. From far off, I heard her say, "And Venarion, of course, was meant to leave the Rise years ago and come here in the Star-ship. But he never did. He hasn't, alas, the guts Argul has, has he, Venarion? That wretched Narsident—what Venarion might have been, with *another* father."

Can you follow this? I can't. Or, I can, but don't want to.

Then she said this.

"In a way, I do think of you, too, as nearly my daughter—Claidi. The ones who are valuable, the ones who rebel—who have stamina, cheek, courage, imagination—passion. Like Argul. Like *You*. Oh, my dear, in the end it doesn't matter to us that you're slave-born. You have passed all the tests. You have the magic spark. Look what you've done! Smashed the City Law—dared the Star-ship—and even after we forced the Star to come down, to test you further—"

"*You* forced—the Star—*down*—"

"Don't fret, you were wonderful. On you journeyed. Then came the panther that talked. Another doll of ours, one of our very best—do you remember, it even smelled as if it had been eating meat? It guided you. You showed no fear. You followed your instructions. And then when you found Argul, as you thought, you would not be put off. *Wouldn't* give up."

"Suppose I had?" I gasped.

"Then," she said. She smiled a dark little smile. "You'd have been worthless."

"Thanks."

"But you see, at last we have too-near-perfect pairings. You, with Argul. My own—er, Winter—with Venarion. Argul is superior and will make up for any weakness of yours. My daughter is superior and will do the same with Venarion. Two glorious chances."

"For what?"

"Ustareth and I were exceptional women, in our day. As our own mothers have been, the Old Ladies Jizania and Ironel. You and my daughter, Venarion and Argul, are also exceptional. From such a line—your children—what will they be?"

I stared at her. "Our *children*."

"Think. The Wolf Tower is our enemy, we are united in that. But some of us too have Wolf Tower blood. Even Argul has it." Speechless, I watched her glowing there. "Do you know about wolf packs, the real wolves? Only the best among them may become leader—the king or the queen. Only these royal animals are allowed to mate."

"You're saying that if Argul and I have a child—"

"The Future," she said. She was radiant as the lamps. "The Future must shine. You are a heroine, Claidi, and Argul is a hero. Think what your *child* would be."

"Give us a chance," I said wearily. "We haven't even met for about a year."

"My dear, you wondered why they applauded you in Chylomba. This is why. You will one day be the mother of a very great woman—"

"Or *man*—"

She ignored me. "You will be the mother," she decided, "of a Queen of the Wolves."

After she swept out—and she did sweep, like a *broom*—I sat there. Now I couldn't think at all.

Then, in the end, I looked up.

In the icy dark of the star-pinned window, a man was standing, on the windowsill *outside*—about a hundred feet up from the ground.

"WE"

Jelly . . . !"

I was rushing to the window to try to open it and get him in before he plummeted down the Tower—and not knowing *how* the window opened—when it opened.

Jelly sprang through into the room.

The window shut.

I thought, insanely, He's shorter. Taller than me, but not so tall as he was—not seven feet tall—his skin is darker—much— he's *tanned* in the snow—? Why is he striding right at me?

Jelly caught me in his arms without a word.

As his mouth met mine I stopped flailing.

His mouth on mine, I knew who he was.

Into my ear he whispered, "Keep your eyes shut. Say *Darling*—"

"Darling—"

"Now listen. I know they have science here and can watch and see a lot. In this room too. Hear us as well, maybe. But hopefully not this, me whispering in your ear. Say *Darling*—"

"*Darling*—"

"So I can't tell you much now. If I put you off when you ask a question—will you trust me?"

"Darling—"

"Good. The thing is, agree with me, but make it convincing."

"Er—*what*, darling?"

"Make it look as if I talk you around. Do you agree? If you agree, say my name."

"Argul," I said.

"Best bird," he breathed.

He let me go.

There he was. And there Jelly wasn't. "Jelly" had been only Argul's disguise.

"Claidi," he said.

"I—I'm not sure I can be called Claidi, anymore."

"Claidi-baa-baa then," he said, "a sheep in wolf's clothing."

I started to giggle. Started to cry. Got myself in order. Unmistakable. No doll, but flesh and blood, and alive. Argul. *Here*.

In fact, I think he *has* grown taller. He's eighteen—nineteen now? I suppose maybe he has. His hair is growing through quickly.

The chemical thing he now tells me he took (more of

Ustareth's sorcery) to make his tea-dark skin so pale and rough, and which also made him lose weight, is wearing off. The built-up long false chin he wore broke when the doll-Argul punched him. The swollen bruise replaced it. But chin and bruise have now vanished, along with all the bandages which were also a disguise. And he's removed the pouches from around his eyes.

The boots with extra inches on the soles—half a hand's height, he says—these made him so much taller and his feet look colossally big. They're also gone. They made him walk oddly, so he exaggerated that. He had known the Towers would be watching. There could be spies . . . everywhere.

"Your hand was so cold that time at Panther's Halt."

"I was scared frozen," he says.

"Of the spies?"

"You," he says. "I know you're trouble."

He's telling me quite a lot, though. So these things must now be safe for the Raven Tower to know we know.

Are they listening? Watching? As I stare and stare at him, my one true love. NO ONE will ever make me think only some gadget brought me to be with him.

He's been so close to me all this while.

"I had to disguise myself, Claidi. Even from you. I didn't want to involve you too soon. I didn't know who was a spy, *darling,*" he adds, to remind me we still don't know who our friends are but must make out we think we're safe here. "These Raven people," he adds, *looking* at me, "*darling,* they're to be trusted."

"Are they?"

It was easy to sound unsure.

"Oh, they're fine," he says. "Would I lie?"

"Well," I overact, "if *you* say so—"

"Well done," he says.

"But," even now I have to ask, "why that name—*Jelly*—that thing about being molded and set by the Wolf Tower—you said you were a Wolf Tower man!"

"I am," he says. "If Ustareth was my mother."

"How did you—" can I ask this? "—how did you learn?"

"Ironel told me," he firmly says. He looks sternly down his nose, the way I remember.

"But Argul—" I suddenly stammer—"Twilight Star—she wants to breed us—like graffs—like vrabburrs—"

"*Darling.* Come on. *Not* like that. Ironel explained to me about Twilight and Ustareth's Dream-plan. You just don't understand yet."

Pretend, he is saying. I choke. I say, humble, "No?" Feeling *them* listen.

"Raven Tower is clever. They have plans, but they're good plans. After all—you don't mind being with me?"

"Put like that . . . when *you* say it—" I gooily add, "it sounds heavenly."

He is holding my hands in his. He looks at them and says, "You weren't wearing the ring I gave you. Now you are."

I thought of Blurn, accusing me of not wearing Argul's ring. "I was just—"

Argul says, "Darling, please *keep* wearing it."

Before I can make a decision if that is to do with the Towers, or that, well, he wants me to wear the ring—*again* someone knocks.

Probably just as well. My acting was getting superuseless.

But yes, they must have listened. Known he was here and who he is, at last.

The door flies wide.

All of them were now with us.

Ngarbo and five other men escorted them, very brave and ready. Twilight was first, with Winter walking right behind her. Then a man.

Argul bowed. "My Lady Princess Twilight Star! Lord Fengrey Raven!"

Fengrey? Since Argul seemed to know everything, I assumed it must be.

Fengrey Raven was stocky and muscular, with lion-colored skin, and black hair in a long tail high on his head. A terrific face, slanting eyes which were green—He looked quite serious, and nodded, as Twilight smiled, all charm.

But Winter pounced into the room.

"And *I* am?"

She'd always thought she would get to marry Argul.

Argul looked at her. "Um? Sorry . . ." ever so confused.

"Madam," said Ngarbo, "that isn't the prisoner, Jelly. Or, it was. He's altered."

"He was in disguise," said Twilight, "weren't you? How intelligent. We heard of this alarming Jelly—none of us knew it to be you. I am impressed, Argul. But not surprised."

"Argul? Be careful, lady," said Ngarbo. "He gets violent, this Argul."

"Only when escaping *you*," commented Argul.

Ngarbo scowled, touching his cut lip. "Right. How did you manage *this* time? That prison window was a mile high."

"I'm fair at climbing," said Argul, modest.

"You're a *mountain-deer* at climbing, *and* in the town. I—"

Winter broke in. "You fooled them, *Argul*. You even fooled me. Jelly. Quite a victory. So sorry about tying you up. I'm Claidi, by the way."

"Really?" Argul, polite.

"He seems to know about all that," said Twilight.

I looked at Fengrey. He hadn't spoken.

Then he did.

"You must dine with us, tonight."

His voice, and what he said, were dull. He sounded much older than he looked. Old and worn-out and—uninterested.

Well, those two, T and W, must be rather exhausting.

Winter crossed the room. She looked up at Argul. "Yes, you're spectacular," she said. "But I shall prefer Venarion."

Argul gave a yack of laughter. Stopped it and bowed again.

I never saw him bow— as himself—till today. Hulta don't. Or have I just forgotten?

If I didn't know, hadn't held him in my arms—would I wonder now if this is yet another doll—another trick—?

Can I trust—him?

Yes.

He trusted me. Not once has he said, Did you want Nemian?

Winter somehow was ruling the scene.

She stood between us, Argul and me.

"Has she told you all her adventures, *your* Claidi here?" inquired Winter Raven.

"Ironel told me," said Argul.

"Oh? About the Rise and all that too? About Prince Venarion—*she* calls him Venn, of course. She knows him well."

A wave of fire went through me. I felt myself go red. This is just wonderful—out of the soup-pan into the stew-pot.

"I heard about Venarion," said Argul. He didn't seem uneasy, angry. But maybe, if he has heard about Venn—maybe he *is* uneasy and angry and only hiding it from them, or from me—or—

Winter put her arm through Argul's. She took a step, meaning them to go on a walk, I suppose, around the large room arm-in-arm. But Argul didn't move when she did, and so *she* nearly fell over. Covered it well, beaming up at him.

"If you get tired of her," said Winter, "I'm sure there are lots of Raven girls who would like to spend time with you. Not me, obviously, I'm spoken for. By Venn. Venn can be very possessive—did you find that, Claid?"

In the doorway, Ngarbo and the other guards were blank. Twilight was smiling and smiling, enjoying this—probably still testing us all, to see how we matched up. (But they all do this, Tower people.)

Fengrey yawned.

I said, "It's such a shame no one ever told Venn that you were waiting here for him, Lady Winter, so loyally. I'm sure he'd have rushed to find the Star-ship and been over the sea to you like a shot."

"Yes," she said. "But *you* were supposed to be me. Enough to put anyone off me, if it was *you*."

Catty and underhanded.

But she had left Argul; she was standing with me now.

"Shall I tell her?" she asked herself. She considered. She said, "Remember that letter Venarion was sent, a flying letter, he called it. It said what a nuisance you were, Claidi, how you'd caused problems everywhere. Then insisted on being sent to him, and he shouldn't believe anything you said, you were a practiced liar. It quite put him off you, didn't it, for a while?"

I stared at her.

"When I found out," said Winter, suddenly low and fierce, "that old Ironel, the interfering old bag, had sent you to him—*him*, Venarion—*my* Venarion—well." Her voice loosened and was playful again. "I naughtily sent him that letter. I signed it 'We'—do you recall? That sounded just like an upper authority of the Towers. *We. We*—was me, Claidi, and it serves you right."

How odd. Her tone all light and spiteful and satisfied. Her eyes full of tears.

She's been hurt. Really hurt. By the Towers—Wolf, Raven, whoever. Hurt like all of us.

I looked down. When I looked up again, her eyes were dry. She was dancing off to flirt with Ngarbo, who seemed pleased, the total dope.

Twilight was leading Argul away too, and he was letting her.

I had to trust him.

Agree to things.

Fengrey looked back at me and nodded, stifling another yawn. "Until dinner, madam."

"Oh, whatever shall I wear?" I dimly tweeted, feeling completely shattered. (She—had been—"*We*.")

"Better to think," said Fengrey bleakly, "of your wedding gown."

Did I say shattered? *Now* I was shattered.

I must have looked about sixteen question-marks at him. My mouth, naturally, fell open.

"You're to be married to Argul; I gather it should have happened before, but the Wolf Tower intervened. Now Twilight would like you wed as soon as possible. In the next couple of days."

"I see."

"Good evening," said Fengrey. Off he stalked, his embroidered coat and hair-tail swinging. (So I thought of the talking doll-panther in the forest and abruptly suspected it had had Fengrey's bored voice!)

Writing this now, I wonder if *they* will try to read my diary. Why not? They pry into everything else. So, it stays with me at all times, both books. They usually do anyway. And when I sleep, I shall tie them to me, around my waist. That'll be *really* comfortable.

THE OVER-MARRIAGE

All that was yesterday. This morning they brought my wedding dress. It reminds me most of the clothes I had to wear in the Wolf Tower.

Very stiff, the skirt so narrow I can hardly take a step, with a pattern like layers of silver feathers. A huge fanned-out collar sewn with pearls. There's also a headdress of lots of little glass drops. And—glass shoes. Well, they look like glass. I can see my feet through them, carefully tended, each with a flower drawn on, and my toenails painted silver.

I've only seen Argul when other people were there. Like at dinner last night, in what they call Hall Three.

Elaborate dishes of food, every mouthful tasting of something different (and odd). A huge fireplace shaped like an open mouth, with fangs. (Yuk.)

House ravens did tricks. Feathers in everything.

There was some dancing, too. Argul and I danced now and then—they asked/told us to. But they were always those dances where every other step you change partners. . . . We only ever seemed to get to dance that kind.

Winter only danced when it was a one-to-one dance, and then she danced with everybody, *except* Argul. She even got her father to dance with her. After that Fengrey went off with most of the older men, to play cards in another room.

Argul *seemed* completely at ease. Not ecstatic exactly, but—content. But Argul is a master of disguise of every sort.

I kept quiet. Seemed the best idea.

Only once, when we had half a second alone by a window, I said, "Can't we get out of here? I mean, get away?"

"There's a good reason to stay."

"Which is?"

But Twilight had by then sailed up, smiling her smile, wanting us to meet and "spend a moment" with some important Old Ladies of the Raven Tower.

I kept thinking, he had escaped them several times, run rings around them. He'd come into the Tower to be with me, protect me as best he could. But was I now holding us both back? After all, unlike him, I didn't think I'd be much use at climbing up and down the Tower.

They let us (told us to) kiss good night on a staircase (nonmoving) watched by about ninety people, who *clapped* and cried "By the Raven!" (Double yuk.)

But under the noise, I said to him quickly, "Are we trapped?"

"No," he said. Then, *"Darling"*—our warning code word now—*"Darling,* you said you'd trust me."

So *"Darling,* I do," I gooed.

I couldn't sleep. I kept wondering if Argul would suddenly appear again at the window somehow. But obviously he would-n't risk the climb now, and he is watched. Why must we *stay?*

The wedding dress and shoes—all fit perfectly. To them, getting that sort of thing right is simple.

One extra thought. *Me* getting something right. I asked for some thread, ripped up a petticoat, and sewed a pocket in the lining of the dress, down by the hem, for both these books to go in when I wear it. And if they "watched" that, let them.

Apparently it's tomorrow. The wedding.

An unappetizing man, called the Wedding Controller, came and lectured me on how I must behave during the Ceremony.

I never thought I would ever dread marrying Argul.

Now I do.

The marriage is in Hall Four.

But—Hall Four is *very* special.

Hall Four—is in the sky.

I should have been prepared for anything. I thought I was.

Once the maids had gotten me ready, I was escorted up to a terrace high up around the side of the Tower. (We went by moving stair.)

I thought this terrace was Hall Four, and was very put off,

because it was in the open air. But crowds of people were there, all massively overdressed. Little trays of sweets and beetles and other muck were going around. It wasn't snowing, but freezing cold under the grim damson sky.

I couldn't see Argul.

Craning about, I tried to. I thought frankly he'd spot me first, as of all the overdressed herd I *was* probably the worst. I stood there, in the slim-line, overwide-collared dress and hair-thing—like some sort of sparkly Peshamban toffee-apple.

"It's thought unlucky," said Twilight, abruptly beside me, "for the groom to greet the bride before the wedding."

"That's why he's hiding from me?"

"Yes. You must hide from him, too."

"Quite a challenge, in this outfit."

She looked *lovingly* at me. Even my sarcasm was being measured and approved.

All this time, because of what Argul had said to me, I'd been trying to be adorable with Twilight. But whenever I met her—my skin crawled.

She looked glorious. What else? Her dress was scaled crocodile green.

"I haven't been able to prepare you for the ceremony," she said. "I think the Wedding Controller gave you some instruction?"

"Yes, thanks."

I thought of the stick he'd kept slapping repeatedly on his boot, instead, I felt, of where he'd like to slap it—on my hands. But the wedding was simple enough. Just another case of doing as I was told

Among the Hulta, one of the Old Men would have married Argul to me, and an Old Woman would have married me to Argul.

Here it was apparently to be Lord Fengrey who would marry us, at the altar of the Tower god.

That had sort of surprised me. In the House, and in the Wolf Tower, there had been no gods, and seldom mention, that I ever heard, of God. (In the House, never even that.)

The way the Controller spoke of this god, though, it/he/she didn't seem to amount to much—just some ritual object. (Although they seem to swear by it.)

I hoped they'd do the marriage soon. Wanted it over.

But I knew really, being a Tower, the marriage would be extreme in every way. Should I have guessed how extreme?

Some servants came marching along the shivering terrace, bearing what I thought was another, very big, tray.

I didn't ask what it was, but what it turned out to be was something that they had to put down in front of me, and onto which I had to step. So, on I got.

And I didn't say to her, either, Why am I standing on a great big tray? No doubt some other ritual, which the Wedding Controller had forgotten to tell me about.

Then something strange. There were now four Raven Guards standing, two either side of the tray. They were attaching themselves to the tray, by shoulder-harnesses, and long chains that went through the sides of it.

Ngarbo was there, and as the chains pulled taut, he said, "Please grasp two of the chains, lady, and hold very tight."

I had time to think, That sounds like the moving stair again; they must be going to pick me up and carry me—

When—

Now I was a silver toffee-apple with her mouth hanging wide open in disbelief. But it was handy to have my mouth open, because in a minute I was going to want to scream my head off.

One by one, then in groups, in clusters, the people on the terrace—were *rising up into the air.*

They rose with the ease of blown soap bubbles. Weightless, smooth.

Some of them were even laughing and talking on together. So I almost thought—Do they know what's *happened* to them?

And then—oh—we—*we* were going up too.

The four guards were lifting upward. The tray lifted quite steadily and effortlessly between them. Not even really a jolt.

I saw the terrace leave their feet. Their feet leave the terrace. The terrace sank away and away and *away.*

We were in midair.

All around us, relaxed people, rising through the sky, still having idiot conversations, of which I heard snatches. "Oh, I *do* like your sash." "Have you *seen* Maysel's *hair?*" "Oh confound it, look, I dropped my glass."

They can fly. Somehow I had thought it would be like birds. . . . Why would it? They don't have wings.

No, they "fly" merely by *rising off the ground,* going up and up—and since I can't, they have to carry me, on a tray—

Where is Argul? On another tray? Did he *know* about this—if he did, why didn't he warn me—

In the crowd, the rising flying crowd—I still couldn't see him. And now low clouds were swirling around us, like fog.

I'd been in the Star and seen clouds wrap around the ship. But *in* the Star. Safe inside.

"It's all right, lady," said Ngarbo. "We won't drop you."

Was it mockery—or a thoughtful reassurance?

It can't have taken long. A few minutes. I'll never forget it. That rising, clutching two of the chains, seeing these overdressed, chattery people floating up with me, through a fog of cloud, their crystal goblets and jewels glinting. And every so often, the colossal walls of the mountains glimpsing through all around, so huge and far off and *near* all at once—

I thought I'd be sick.

Was looking around and down at who I thought I'd like best, of the ones rising up below me, to be sick *on*—when Ngarbo said, "See, we're there."

No longer rising, they were all taking weird swimming *steps* forward—walking now, in the sky. Something loomed, warmer, bright—we *were* there.

The tray grounded. Ngarbo took my arm to stop me falling flat on my face. My chest felt tight. I was dizzy.

Someone else had my other arm.

"That was a rotten trick—she didn't tell you about that, did she? My mother can be a real so-and-so."

Blearily I turned and saw my arch-enemy, Winter Raven, was helping hold me up. She wore gold striped with black—and looked like a wasp.

I shook her off. Stood straight.

"No, I think she did somehow forget to mention it."

"It's these," said WR. She pointed at her amber necklace. "And her turquoise. We all have jewelry that can do it. Lift us up, get us down. They have magnets in them."

That was like the Star. Yinyay had said—the ship's magnets reacted to gravity, absorbing and canceling it to let the Star rise, gradually reintroducing it to let the Star land.

Why was WR being friendly and sympathetic? Some new plot—

I turned. Argul was there.

Even in a state, I saw he looked amazing. All in scarlet and gold, his still-short hair gleaming black silk, his skin tea-dark again. But he was strained, his eyes wide on me.

"Are you all right, Claidi?"

"Are you?"

"That was either meant," he said, "to be a brilliant thrill for us—or a big smack in the gob."

She spoke, "Smack in the gob."

"Well, you'd know," he said.

"All right," she said, "I am *sorry* about the other day. But look—I'd have at least *told* you about this beforehand. I don't like the games they play either, you know. My mother, my father—when he can be bothered. They mess me about, too. I've had seventeen years of it."

Green crocodile Twilight was there.

"Now you *can* be together, my dears," she said to Argul and me. "It's quite all right."

"No one told them about the flight up," said Winter.

"Really? I'm sure someone was meant to. . . ."

I saw Argul give her his first unliking look. She raised her brows.

Up here—for the first time, standing beside him, I looked around. I mean, where on earth—where *off* earth—were we?

We'd come in through an arch, very tall and wide. There was a floor of tiles, dark and gleaming. If it hadn't been for the shine of the lamps and candles on their stands, the shine of them in the glass walls of the great chamber—I might have thought we were just balanced on one more tray, up in the air.

The high ceiling was glass too, but mirror. Everything and everyone was reflected up there. Staring up, I looked into my own far-off upturned face.

At the other end of the long room, a great fountain. Even I could see it wasn't water. Out the spouts in the beaks of white stone birds, from the held-high trumpets of white stone people, gushed gushes of something tinted every color in the world.

"Air fountains," said Winter Raven. "It's necessary. The air's thin up here, you see." (I was relieved I hadn't just been panting from being cowardly.)

I thought, Hrald would *love* this.

I thought, How does this glass room stay put? Like the Star-ship, maybe. More magnets, of course.

I've never understood about those magnets. And I wasn't going to ask now.

Argul was there, and I could feel the warmth and strength of him, and when he took my hand, it *was* him. Not any trick—

Only, there had been so many tricks. Even he—had tricked

me, misled me. He'd had to, he'd said. To fool the ones who *watched*.

Even so.

I hadn't known him—at Panther's Halt, the Hills, Ice-Walk, Chylomba—all that time I'd ridden after Argul, only it hadn't been him but a mechanical doll. And meanwhile he, disguised as Jelly, had ridden after *me*.

Now musicians were starting to play a stately tune. The crowd drew aside, leaving an open lane. At the top of this lane of people, exactly in front of the gushing air fountain, I now saw what must be the altar. It was a stone thing with a black stone raven. Lord Fengrey was there. Looking bored but resigned.

The Wedding Controller appeared.

"Now then," he clucked, tapping his posh stick on his boot.

So. Argul and I must walk up the aisle, between the staring people of the Raven Tower. Up the aisle of the room in the sky. And when we came to the stone altar, Lord Fengrey would marry us. (If he hadn't nodded off from uninterest.)

We walked, in time to the slow music, as the Wedding Controller had just told us we should. Twilight and Winter walked behind us, but not very close.

Argul spoke to me, under the music.

"This is it, Claidi."

"Yes."

"I don't mean this tronk of a marriage. I mean, Claidi, you are really going to have to trust me—Claidi—listen, whatever I tell you to do, *do* it. Will you?"

"Yes, Argul."

"You don't know what I'm going to ask, Claidi."

"No. Something—difficult."

"See that bird thing on the altar?"

"Their Raven god—is it—?"

"In a way. When we get there, put your hand out, the hand with your diamond ring I gave you. Don't let them stop you. Right?"

"My hand with the diamond . . ."

"Touch the raven."

"Why?"

"Claidi, though I love the way you always ask questions at the wrong moment, now is the wrong moment plus."

"But—"

"Touch the raven. It may spit or something. Don't worry."

"Spit—is it alive?"

"Claidi—no, it's not alive. Just touch it."

"Yes, Argul."

"Do you want them to marry us?" he abruptly added.

It was a long way to the altar. The music we must keep time to made the walk very slow. It helped muffle what we said.

People were laughing on both sides, or laughing *at* us.

I could smell the strange acid smell of the air fountain.

"Don't you want to marry me anymore, Argul? I—I thought you still did."

"I don't want *this* load of morbofs to do it. God, Claidi. They overdo everything. Their rituals, their *games*—their clothes. We wouldn't be married, we'd be—"

"Over-married."

"Right. Claidi-baa-baa, we'll marry, but somewhere else."

I could see Fengrey so clearly now, standing there, piled

with robes, at the altar. This bored, overdressed man—I didn't want him to have anything to do with us. And T and W lurking at our shoulders. And—breeding us, as Ustareth bred her peculiar animals. Let's face it, as Venn had almost said—Ustareth bred *herself*, too, to see what she would get. (I) Venn—not good enough. (2) Argul—a success!

"When you've touched the stone raven," said Argul, "I want you to do just one more thing."

"Yes, Argul?"

"Jump over the fountain."

"—Argul? It's about ten man-heights high, isn't it?"

Suddenly this explosion of women in frothy dresses boiled out of the crowd, singing and chucking flowers, and we were surrounded.

"*Darling*," growled Argul violently.

So I knew I mustn't ask another thing.

OUT OF THE CAGE

We had reached the altar.

The music ended. The crowd went quiet. I could hear only the gush of the fountain, and the spat-spat of flames in the real lamps.

I turned and looked up at him. And in that second he drew a knife that maybe they—and certainly I—didn't know he had in his wedding finery.

Fengrey's noble mindless face—swelled as if about to pop.

I reached forward and gripped the head of the raven statue on the altar. I used both hands, in case.

A spray of sparks!

I staggered back, wondering if I was on fire or had been struck by lightning.

"*Jump*, Claidi!" Argul shouted.

I think I knew. It wasn't only that I trusted him. Perhaps I didn't trust him, not even Argul, right then.

But the diamond ring, which had seemed to have such odd powers at the Rise—the diamond was blazing heatless blinding white—a firework.

So—I jumped. Right for the top of the fountain, sixty feet up in the ceiling.

Then *I* was in the ceiling. I was up there, by the mirror— I shrieked as I saw my own reflection rush toward me—a screaming young woman in a silver dress and too many pearls— and just as I thought I'd strike her head-on, smash her and die—the whole roof opened like the petals of an obliging rose—

And *then* I was arrowing on into the plum-black cloud—and then Argul grabbed me.

"It's all right. Down now—we're too high."

"But Argul—you're flying too—"

"You bet."

I found we were quite still. Hanging there in midair, midcloud.

Ridiculous to the last, I noticed I'd split the skirt of the silver dress.

"How have we stopped?" I asked.

"You meant to stop, and so did I. That stops us. But we should get down lower. This air's too thin."

"What do I—"

"Tell it down, or *think* down. Either."

Yes. The ring reacted to thought, didn't it. Oh . . .

We dropped, quite quickly but not frighteningly so, and the cloud dissolved.

It was—too mad—too *dream*like to be scary now. Although—I must be scared.

"Argul, how can *you* fly?"

"Later, Claidi-baari."

He veered away, and I found I was veering with him.

Incredible—

We whizzed through a gulley between two towering crags that gleamed in their armor of snow. Behind, over there, that white-capped dark thing *far down* was the *head* of the Raven Tower. (Up against the cloud, I couldn't see the glassy bubble of Hall Four.)

Now Argul was landing like a splendid scarlet eagle on a ledge. So—I landed there too. Faultlessly. Then I sat down with a bump. (If I fell right off, it wouldn't matter, would it?)

"We haven't long," he said. "Look."

I peered back into reeling distance. A flight of bats was circling out against the snows.

"They're coming after us."

"What else? Most of the Tower Guard can fly, and all the nobles. Let's make this fast."

We dashed up again. Into the air I thought what good targets we'd present. I in the flashy silver and he in the red. Could they shoot—as it were—on the wing?

I thought—But we are *flying*.

How? Why? What is going on?

We went so fast now. Too fast to think. I simply did what I'd seen him do. Where he dipped, looped, I did. The freezing wind hissed in our faces. My headdress finally came undone and blew away behind me.

It wasn't like that tray with chains—I could even look down—as if I'd done this before . . . or as if the ring knew and had told me—

But when I turned I saw *them*, those dark shapes—they no longer looked like birds or bats—they were *running* through the air.

It isn't flying. I too was doing this running thing, like Argul. We were leaping on and on, upright, not lying flat on the air, and holding our arms in to our bodies.

We raced around a tall white spire that looked almost like a terrible face. Spinning in, I came up on another ledge and this time didn't sit down. Argul landed beside me.

"The ring," I said.

"It does what it's supposed to," he said.

We were both gasping from the scanty high mountain air, the cold and rush, the escape. I said, "If we keep running, they may keep on chasing. They may catch us. This ring—I think maybe, though I can't know—I think it can protect us. What I'm saying is, it has more powers than flight. What do you think?"

He looked at me. He smiled. He said—*he* said—"I'm in your hands."

The flank of the mountain still hid our pursuers. Yet I could feel them getting near.

At the Rise, the diamond had done the wildest things, not all helpful. And then in the end it hadn't worked at all. But as I looked at it now, it glowed up like an icy sun, answering my unspoken thought. Whatever the ring had been before, now it was itself. And *mine*.

In case I made a mistake, I said the words aloud. "The ones chasing us, don't let them take us. Even if they get within arm's length—keep them off. Please."

The ring flared a beam of white fire.

Will it work?

It had to.

And—it did.

As we stood there, crammed in against the wide of the mountain, out of the bottomless snow-corridors of the upper air came sky-running the Guards of the Raven Tower.

They burst around the mountain, circled in space a moment, calling to each other.

I saw Vilk, and another one I recognized, seven more, then Ngarbo. None of them looked anymore like anyone I'd ever known or would ever want to. Their faces were hard and changed. But they glared—*right at us.*

Now they'll fire. Can the ring deflect bullets?

They didn't fire.

It was Vilk who dived over to the shelf of rock where we stood. As he clutched our bit of mountain with one hand, his eyes met mine—looked *through* mine.

He cursed and dropped away. "Only a damned shadow."

And so I knew.

Invisible. We were invisible.

"Come on, Vilk!" Ngarbo shouted. "Why are you wasting time?"

Vilk veered off.

They stormed by, and after them swirled another ten, twenty men, all looking around, looking right through us. Furious not to find us, angry ravens against the grey-white crags. Then only small as birds again, bats, flies. Blind—to us. They were gone. Silence closed behind them.

There was a cave we'd found. We were sitting in it. I'd tried the ring, and the ring had made a neat bright fire for us with one mild wink.

Perhaps oddest of all, I was already used to the ring, to asking it to do things—astonishing things—and having them done.

"You say please and thank you every time," said Argul.

"I prefer to."

"You have a good heart," he said. And I thought of Venn's grating comments on my thanking of doll-servants and Yinyay in the Star.

We were warm in the cave, but outside darkness was falling. Then it got light again—white thick snow was coming down.

Argul had brought some food for us. He had known we'd be leaving the Tower. (I, of course, had only sensibly brought these books. Oh, and Dagger's dagger.)

Once, we heard more of *them* go by outside. Or the first lot coming back to double-check. Our fire shone in the cave-opening, and they didn't see it. I don't know how the ring does this. The main thing is, it does.

We sat on his marriage cloak.

"I suppose the ring can't summon some pillows?" asked Argul

"It might—but they'd have to come from somewhere,

wouldn't they, and pillows flying in the air might be a give-away—"

"True. This rock is nice and soft, after all."

He put his arm around me. He said, "I can try to answer all your million questions now, Claidi."

But somehow, we waited a while for the questions.

They are so arrogant, the people of the Towers. Wolf, Tiger, Vulture, Pig, Raven. The Houses too, with their names like Sea-View and Holly Trees.

The women are the worst, the ones I've met. The Old Ladies, like Ironel and Jizania. And the princess-ladies like Twilight Star, who I'm so glad *isn't* my mother.

But it's science-magic and power that makes them so deadly.

Am I now going to turn into someone like that?

I must watch myself, every inch of the way. But he's there too. Argul. To anchor me to the earth. To give me wings of the heart.

The answers to the other questions? I'm going to write them out. Hope I don't miss anything. You've been very patient.

THE RINGS

I thought it was best to write about them first.

Argul, who told me all this, knows everything *he* does because Ironel told him everything *she* knew. Which was quite a lot. But I'll come to that in a minute.

Ustareth-Zeera made two or three rings, all with great powers. Later she was able to put these powers, or some of them, into other sorts of jewelry as well—necklaces, pendants, and so on.

Her main reason was selfish. She *liked* to experiment—I think we all know *that* by now. But she was also a genius.

She left her *topaz* ring at the Rise for two reasons: (1) For Venn, if he could be bothered to look for it, but (2) because it had more or less stopped working. It was an early model. And its power ran out—rather the way a candle will burn down.

Meanwhile she'd made the diamond ring, and this she took with her. Among all the other things it could do, the diamond had—as we've seen—the power to give its wearer flight—by which I mean she can defy gravity, traveling at any preferred height and speed.

That was how she got through the jungle, got across the sea. Under those circumstances she hadn't needed her Star-ship. So she left that for Venn too—again, if he had the brains and spirit—or rashness—to search it out.

Maybe even then she did hope he'd follow her one day. Maybe she was sorry to leave him, only two years old, there in the Rise, with just an Ustareth look-alike doll to be his unloving mother. Until it too broke down.

When Ustareth got with the Hulta and became Zeera, she wanted to be sure her diamond ring was safe from anyone else. So she had it reset in Hulta gold. *That* lessened its powers, or fully shut them off from anyone but her. Which was why, when she died, no one ever thought the diamond was anything more than a beautiful ring. And when Argul gave it to me and I wore it all the time, nothing weird at all happened. (Or if it did, I didn't connect it up.)

Even when I was kidnapped, the ring did nothing. Its power was locked up by the setting, and I had no way to let it out—even if I'd known what it was.

Then though, when I was at the Rise, even when I was on my way there in the jungles she made, the ring sort of began to wake up.

Locked in the cage of its setting, it couldn't work properly, or do anything I really needed.

But all those mechanisms of hers at the Rise set it off all over the place.

In the library, though, the ring *was* able to do things like opening a door, or making the library machines bring me a book. I think her power was very strong in that room. Or, maybe, the ring was just beginning to get used to *me*.

Later in the jungle, when I was with Venn, the topaz didn't work—it had given one slight show of power, rather as a candle might flare up just before it goes out. After that it was spent. The diamond didn't seem to do anything either. When we were attacked by vrabburrs—but then, they were attacking Venn, not me, and I didn't know what I could do—and anyway, we were rescued.

When I came back, I took off the diamond. I didn't trust it. Perhaps if I'd kept it on, tried to—well, talk to it, practice with it—it might have gotten stronger. Or not.

What it really needed was a powerful direct charge from another of Ustareth's machines designed to do exactly that. Something that would get it to work, despite the Hulta setting, full-strength again.

The Raven "god" of the Raven Tower did that. That is where all of them recharge their power-jewelry, if they think it's getting weak. It isn't a god. It's a—well, a sort of—what? All I can think of is, if the fire gets low, you throw on another log. The raven-god is like throwing another log into the fire.

Only, Argul says, now the fire will last in the ring. Last forever. At least, so long as I keep wearing it. It was her *own* ring, you see. The best she ever made.

He'd been told by Ironel the recharging raven was here. Which was why he wanted us to get to the Tower, and stay in the Tower until we found it, or they showed it to us. Argul didn't know, Ironel hadn't, where they kept the wretched thing. Of course they'd put it out of harm's way, up in the air!

Eventually they might, Argul said, have given me the power of the ring—if I was a good girl and showed I was repulsively loyal to them. After all, I was against the Wolf Tower, and Raven Tower is Wolf Tower's number-one enemy.

(Does it go to show that, by trying to be against one bad thing, you can end up as disgusting yourself?)

"Why," I said, "did they ever risk letting us into Hall Four, where the raven was?"

Argul shrugged. "The interesting thing, to me anyway, is that Zeera—Ustareth—my mother, left the ring for my wife. She told me, when I was a child. She said, when I found the woman I wanted, this was the ring she must have."

"Your wife was meant to be Twilight's daughter, Winter," I muttered, scowling.

"Whoever it was, Claidi, that power was meant for her, not me."

But Ustareth-Zeera had left something for Argul, too.

I think I've covered the rings, so I'll say about *that* now.

THE SCIENTIFIC CHARM

When we first met, Argul and I, he looked at a glassy object hung on a string around his neck. Later he'd told me it was a kind of scientific charm his mother gave him, to show him if the woman he wanted was right for him, and he for her. (And, as I learned in the RT, that should have been Winter Raven he was gazing at right then.)

Which I shall ignore. For he and I—are meant to be together.

"Ironel," he now said, "took this out of some box and gave it to me. It somehow sticks to the glassy stuff."

He had taken off the charm by then, there in the cave. Handed it to me. In the center of the glassy bulb was now a dark blue gem. A sapphire, I think. When I touched it, it didn't move.

"*Ironel* gave you this?"

"It's the missing piece—only I never knew anything *was* missing."

Ustareth had left the sapphire with her mother, Ironel, to give to Argul if—brace yourself—he ever had the brains and the spirit—and sheer rash craziness?—to wander into the Wolf Tower.

"Another endurance and brains test," I said.

"Seems so. I passed, anyway. Ironel gave me the jewel, told me to attach it. Then told me what it could do."

"Is it the same as the diamond?"

"No. I said, the main power was for whomever I wanted to marry. For you. This has more limited powers. Like most of the jewels in the Raven Tower. But it did let me fly and open a few windows."

"So that's how—"

How he got away from the Raven Guards—twice. Climbed up a wall of the Guest House, up the Raven Tower itself. He didn't climb. He *flew*.

When they shoved him into a tray to go up to Hall Four, he acted as appalled as I was. As in everything else, he'd never let *them* know a thing, until it was too late for them.

But this explains more than that. It explains how he got to Panther's Halt in time to meet me—he bought his horse *there*, because after that he didn't want any spies to notice what he could really do.

And how he kept sneaking up on me, unseen, unheard—to fool them, but it freaked me out too. Of course, when he was unwatched, he'd risk a short flight for speed. (Disguised as Jelly, they would only watch him at first when he was with me.)

"I wasn't that good at it," he said, "a couple of times I sailed off the ground. When I saw you."

I gawked. "That's why you seemed seven feet tall. But the jewels are easy—they just do what you say—even what you *think* to them."

"Yours does," he said. "Yours is special. Or Claidi, just possibly, *you're* special."

I sat and frowned.

He said, "I don't know. But it seems to me, it's the person involved as much as the jewel. The Raven Tower think that, you know, girl. Why they want you."

When I didn't reply, he didn't go on.

And I think I won't, here.

I did say, "These spies everywhere. You mean men from the Towers."

"I mean almost anything, Claidi. Like the doll-man who looked rather like me—"

"He was your double—"

"Oh come on—"

I said firmly, "You mean there were more of those?"

"There might have been. Ironel said that Ustareth had a scientific formula for making them with likenesses like that. So any man, woman, or child—even an animal—might have been something working for the Raven Tower."

I thought. I said, "Even ravens?"

"Why not. The northlands are full of them. Not all real birds? If you don't know—how *can* you know?"

Spies . . . ravens that aren't ravens. People who aren't—people.

I was afraid of the Wolf Tower once. But this Raven Tower—

At least, because of the diamond, now they can't see or hear or find us. But how far does their filthy controlling web extend? I have so many memories of looking up into some sky—and seeing huge circling black birds. . . .

Let me put down the last of the answers, all I have.

IRONEL/USTARETH-ZEERA/TWILIGHT

Whether it was fair to expect him to, or not, Argul *had* gotten to meet Ironel. (He almost met her before. Perhaps she'd been hoping he would, that time he got me away from the Wolf Tower City.)

I think Ironel is just one of those women who like men better than other females. Nemian she seemed to like. Argul she seems to have liked a lot. Her own daughters—well, she never mentioned them to me. Ustareth, at least, I think Ironel respected. But mainly, Ironel likes playing games.

Argul says, once he'd gotten into the Wolf Tower, she whisked them away upriver, to some out-City estate of hers. A looming house of pale grey walls, leaning right over a lake—as if, he said, it wanted to throw up in it.

Here it was she told him all his own history, and everything she knows about Ustareth, and the Rise. And me. Then she gave him the sapphire and told him about that.

"I felt sorry for her. I knew she was dangerous, Claidi. But what has she got? Nothing. Ustareth made her those false teeth—the pearl ones she can't eat anything with." Argul looked into the fire. "She wears them because they were Ustareth's present. But are they a present—or an unkind joke?"

"Both?"

"Yeah."

Ironel hadn't helped Ustareth during Ustareth's unpleasant marriage to Narsident. When Ustareth was sent off to create the jungles at the Rise, mother and daughter hadn't even written. And they can send flying letters out of machines in walls, so distance was hardly a problem.

Then, when U came back, got with the Hulta and became Zeera, had Argul—then she started to visit people.

"Ironel?" I asked.

"Ironel, and Twilight Star whom she admired for her rebellion over Fengrey."

"Didn't the Hulta notice—was Ustareth often away?"

"Never for long," said Argul. "She used to go off sometimes, she said to get herbs, find minerals. Never more than a day and a night. But she could do it, Claidi. She could cross a whole country in a few hours. She could fly. None of us ever knew that."

We sat and thought of this. Ustareth-Zeera whirling along the sky, to the Wolf Tower, the Raven Tower. Friend to both?

"I know about the plan to breed Top Child, preferably a daughter," said Argul. "A ruling female, like in a wolf pack."

"Men and women are equal," I said. "Wolves have kings, too. Why this *thing* about women?"

"Perhaps my mother," he paused, "didn't agree with you about the equal part."

Ust—Zeera—she *was* Argul's mother.

He had never said all that much about her. He didn't now. But he kept looking away. Into the fire, the shadows. At the thick curtain of white snow falling outside, as if the sky could never make enough.

Ustareth told Ironel all her plan, and Ironel was all for it. But Ustareth didn't trust Ironel entirely. She never revealed to Ironel that Twilight's true daughter, so much part of the plan, wasn't the girl left behind in the House.

Ironel knows plenty. (The Wolf Tower has its own machines and tricks. More than I'd ever come across.) But in some areas she's been fooled as thoroughly as I have.

Twilight and Ustareth kept Twilight's secret. After all, they didn't mean T's real daughter to end up Wolf's Paw. No. She had to be free to marry one of Ustareth's sons, and so produce a Wolf Queen.

[*199*]

"You've wrecked their plans," said Argul.

"I hope so. Unless—"

He said, "If and when, Claidi, no child of ours is going to have to put up with *that*."

"They went to so much trouble, though, to try to put you off me. Snatching me away, giving you a fake diary to convince you I was—scum—"

"It's possible," he now said, "that Ironel was behind that part. She may have thought you'd be more suitably *mated* to Venarion—what do you call him—Venn. That was naturally before she *met* me," he added, not at all modestly, grinning.

Who can be quite sure of anything the Towers do? Only sure it's a game, and how they like to play—

Look at how the Ravens had snatched Hedee Poran, and later Yaz and Hrald—why? To find out about the Rise, I think, and how Ustareth's jungles were doing, even how Venn was. H and Y were doubtless able to tell a lot about me, as well. But also—what a *game*.

Argul said, "The joke is, marrying me, because I'm Ustareth's son, makes you Tower blood. Though to Ironel you're Tower blood already—she thinks you're Twilight's girl. While to Twilight you're just another First-Class Rebel she wants for her cause."

"Yes."

"Did you find, the Hulta didn't say much to you—about Ust—about Zeera?"

"No, they didn't. I thought because I was an outsider."

"The Hulta loved her. Put her on a pedestal. And they were afraid of her. And was I? I don't know. She could be wonderful. She knew the name of every plant and animal and planet. She could crack shells and tiny creatures, a million years old, out of the rocks. She could heal almost any illness. Except her own. No, she wasn't perfect."

"Argul . . ."

"It's all right. I thought so much of her. Still think like that. But she was wrapped up in what she wanted to do. She was a kind of glamorous stranger. After all, she's played her game with me too. Even after she died—she's still been playing with us. All these tests she left—telling one person this part of the puzzle, that person another part—letting—*making* us run around to find things, find each other—and if we didn't, like poor damn Venn—we'd miss them and miss out altogether."

We watched the fire, shadows, snow.

"The Hulta made me leader very young; I was fifteen," he said. "Guess why? Not because I was the leader's son, or fantastically worthy. Because she was my mother. That was her power, even after she was dead."

After a long while, I said, "You do believe Venn wasn't so important to me? That Nemian wasn't ever, really."

"It wouldn't even matter," he said quietly. "I'm yours. You're mine. Whatever we did, that can't change."

"Yes." I sighed.

And what *else* matters, I thought, but that?

The ring makes as much light as I want, so I can see to write. (I can't sleep. So I've sat here writing. Argul *is* asleep. He looks very young. Older too. Strange.)

One major thing I must note here. Despite the stuff I'd heard from Yaz and Hrald about Wolf Tower Law starting up again in the City, Argul says he saw absolutely no sign of it. And when he mentioned the Law to Ironel, she'd leered and said, "The Law is in the wastepaper bin of life." (!)

Right after I wrote that, this ring mended my skirt, which I tore kicking off into flight. I was looking at the tear, wishing I could sew it or something. And there was this sort of tugging, and the ring pulled my hand down over the tear. Which—did itself up. Miraculous. Only thing is, once I fly off in the morning, it'll probably rip again.

If I've wrecked their plans—how is it I have the power ring like a reward?

I'm so confused when I try to think it out. I mean, is it just that Ustareth thought whoever got this ring would do what *she* wanted? Ustareth is dead.

I keep thinking, though, about Twilight, all alive. What is *she* doing? Plotting? Ironel was so leery of Twilight and the RT, she didn't tell me half the truth in her letter, in case they saw it. She lied about Argul, too, to keep him out of their clutches until he was ready for them.

Tomorrow, he and I can fly-sky-run away. But are we then going to be on the run for the rest of our lives?

"Argul, I'm going back to the Tower."

"You're—*where?*"

"The Raven Tower. I don't need you to come with me."

"Wait a minute—"

"I'd rather you didn't. It's—I'd rather handle this alone."

"*Claidi—*"

"*Argul.* Nothing can happen to me. Remember the ring?"

We stood in the cave mouth. The snow had stopped falling. Snow had become instead the whole world under the black granite sky.

"Look, Claidi—"

"Once before, at the Wolf Tower, you trusted me to do something alone. Please, do that again now. I *did* succeed."

"All right then." He let me go.

"Will you be safe?" I then asked. "I mean, without the ring—"

"Yes, Claidi. I'll just about be able to manage."

I turned. Glancing down the precipice, I gulped. Idiot. You can fly.

I flew.

A HUMAN FACE

And then there was a dawn. . . . It was as if never before had the sun come up, and now it did.

Strands of lavender cloud drift away—the dark has parted like an opened door.

The wide sky is rose-peach and glassy lemon-gold—and every mountain, every one of the little, down-there humps of the Ups, stroked over with this eatable light.

Oh, what it is to fly! Running through the air. Better, so much better even than riding in the Star with Yinyay—I heard myself laughing from sheer joy.

Then, high above, I spotted a tiny dark blot that didn't move. Thought it a cloud, realized it wasn't. It was Hall Four, its dark tiled floor barely showing in the sky.

And below—the Raven Tower.

A white raven now. The snow had completely covered it, at last, and frozen solid.

I swooped lower. The ring does everything the moment I think of it.

The Tower might have been deserted. Not a lamp, not a single visible sentry. None of the narrow windows showed up through the icy crust of snow. But then, circling the head of the raven, I found that one great red window I'd seen before from the Road, burning like a ruby.

I knew it was *her* window. Who else, but one of those four fearful women (Jizania, Ironel, Ustareth, Twilight) would make for herself a window like that?

The thing with the ring—perhaps the strangest thing of all—is how I'm *used* to it, what it can do. (It had even made me warm, as I felt the snow-chill outside the cave.)

I remember when Argul first gave it to me, and I said, "It feels like it's part of my hand." Its power, now it works, is like that too. Why? I don't know. It's as if Ustareth made it for me. In a way she did—After all, her second son and I were made for each other. By something. By God? If it isn't too cheeky to say it.

Anyway, as I landed on the outer sill, I knew even Argul's charm with the sapphire could open windows. And besides, the ceiling of Hall Four had opened for my ring. So this fire-ruby window would open too.

And it did.

The chamber inside was all smoky twilight colors; it was the lamps and fire that made it glow red.

She hadn't been asleep. She was sitting in a tall chair, and when I jumped down into the room, she got to her feet. She looked—terrified.

Then she controlled that and was all smiles, all Twilight-Star-smiles.

"Good morning, Claidi—I'm so glad to see you."

My landing had knocked snow off the sill onto her carpet. She glanced at that and gave a little wry frown, sort of, Oh, dear, such a welcome guest, mustn't mention her clumsiness.

"I've come to tell you something," I said.

"My dear, of course. Please do sit."

"It won't take long. By the way, don't bother calling your guards—I imagine your turquoise can do that; it's quite strong, isn't it?"

Her face, empty now. "Yes," she said.

"But you know, I think I'm stronger."

I looked in her eyes. Even now, it wasn't that easy.

"Ustareth's diamond," she said. "Yes, her ring is very powerful. How lucky that he knew, and that now it works for you. What are you going to do, kill me?"

That shocked me. That she'd think it, say it. But they *would* think like that, Tower people.

"No, thanks. This is just a warning."

"I see."

"Do you? I hope you do." I could hear myself. I've heard myself sound like that before, now and then. I hope it's not me, merely an act I can put on. I said, impatient with myself, "If it was so dodgy, me being near the raven in Hall Four, you shouldn't have gotten us to marry there."

She looked affronted. She said, "Marriages always take

place in Hall Four. It would be unthinkable anywhere else. A tradition of the Tower."

"A tradition?" I said. "You mean a *rule?*" She didn't like my saying that. "Look, Twilight Star," I went on, "I don't belong to you, nor does Argul. We won't ever do what you want or be what you'd like—or follow any of your *rules*. But if you leave us alone from now on, we'll give no grief to you."

"What a Hulta phrase!" she cried, *so* amused.

"They say something like it in Peshamba, too. And Ustareth was responsible for Peshamba, wasn't she? So it's also an *Ustareth* phrase."

"Very well. You've put me in my place."

"Stay there then. Stay in your *place*."

"As *you* did, Claidi?"

She'd caught me off guard after all. I blinked at her, and in that moment—

I saw a white spinning shoot away from her. It came off the turquoise hanging at her throat. Right for me. And the air blazed up as if it caught on fire.

And then all the fragments of burnt air fell down like black petals. I watched them. I hadn't felt a thing but silly surprise. The ring—had protected me, saved my life, I truly believe. If I hadn't had the ring, I too might have fallen everywhere, in fine black petals.

"You should be careful with that," I said, "it could go off and hurt someone."

But I was shaking.

I could see that she was, too. Her honey-dark skin was sickly. Her eyes drooped.

"I was unwise," she said. "But at least, now I see what I'd be up against. Excuse me, Claidi. I won't try again."

"No, don't ever try again. That's all I came to say. Keep away from me and mine."

Then she did the final most disgusting thing of all, worse than merely trying to scorch me to cinders. She dropped on her knees in front of me, the way some people do before their God or gods.

"Oh—you *are* She," she said. "You—it's *you*—only second generation—*You* are the Wolf Queen, the daughter of power who is *power*. You. And we didn't even *make* you. You're a common *slave*—"

"Yup," I said, "that's me. A common slave. So long." I rose up lazily and rested in the air. Her wet carpet now had a large burn in it. Serves her right, the cow.

The window, which had shut, opened again to let me out.

I sailed around the side of it. The air was icy, and I needed that to steady me, so the ring let me stay cold.

But as I floated past the raven's white head, I reached the beak. Up there was Winter Raven.

She looked over at me.

"Hey, Claidi. Been giving mother some more trouble?"

"A social call," I said.

I could see she had been playing on the beak, to which she had flown, stamping patterns of footprints in the softer snow.

"Don't rush off," she said, "without saying good-bye."

She wore her feather cloak. She looked forlorn, like a beautiful old child that can't remember properly how to be childish.

I found myself sitting on the raven's beak. She sat beside me. We dangled our legs over the vast gulf beneath, knowing that neither of us need ever fear to fall.

Does she realize her mother is a monster, who a short while ago, tried to kill me? Probably. Does she then think I've killed Twilight? To Winter, all that would be normal? Normal, after all, is only what you're used to.

"She's all right," I said.

"Mother? Oh, yes." Silence. "You're soft," she said. Then, "I'll look after your graff. He's nice. They always are. I might mate him to *my* graff." I must have pulled a face. She said, "He won't *mind*, Claidi."

"No, I suppose not."

"And—Argul's horse—I'll take care of that, too."

From the corner of my eye—she's blushing? *Winter?*

"Winter, look—Ustareth used this ring to cross the sea. Would your necklace be strong enough to let you do that?"

She stared at me.

I said, "You know how to find Venn. You sent him a letter there. So, couldn't you just go and *meet* him? He *is* gorgeous," I added temptingly, and generously. "Why don't you talk to Heepo—Hedee Poran, at the Guest House. He knew Venn when Venn was a child. He could fill you in a bit on the situation. I don't see that she—your mother—will stop you. She *wants* you to team up with Venn. Only, I think you have to do it *your* way, not hers."

Winter said nothing, only looked away suddenly. We both did.

We stared down and down into the gulf that had no fear for either of us. No, it was just life—our futures—that were scary.

"Claidi," she said, "I said I was sorry about the way I went on. And that letter, full of lies. Well, there's something else."

My heart sank and my stomach rose. They collided with a bang somewhere around my waist. "Really?" I idly asked.

"She—mother—wanted me to Tag your diary-book. So if you went off any time, they could keep track of you."

"Right."

"The Wolf Tower did it, didn't they, put a Tag in your diary. That yukko Nemian, or someone."

"Yes."

"Look, let's get this straight. I'm not afraid of my mother. She wouldn't hurt *me*. But—I've gotten used to obeying her, and it takes a lot to say No."

"Right."

"I don't think, now that your ring works for you, Tagging the diary would matter anyhow—the ring would just conceal you—perhaps let you know to look for the Tag. But Claidi. I would like you to know. I *didn't* do it anyway.

"No?"

"*No.*"

"Was that only because you couldn't get *near* my book?"

She smirked. "I *knew* you'd say that. No, Claidi, I got near it."

I thought how I'd kept both books close, even before I'd really become supercareful. Slept on the bag they were in, finally tied them to me.

"How?"

"Not saying. I have to keep a few secrets. You know about everything else about me. But get the ring to check the diaries. You'll find I didn't Tag either book. *But* I left you proof I'd gotten at them. I wanted you to know I behaved with—honor."

I stood up. "What's the proof then?"

She told me.

I said, "If that's true, then that means you read my diary."

She, too, rose. She confronted me. "No, it does not. My amber necklace can do stuff too. It *scanned* your diary, looking for a suitable name, and then—well, what I said. *I* haven't read a word. I swear, by the Raven in Hall Four."

"*That* isn't a god."

"By Venn then," she said flamboyantly. "By gorgeous Prince Venarion Yllar Kaslem-Idoros, whom I'm going to meet across the sea."

Will you? I thought. *Will* you go? Just—*do it.*

We shook hands, slipped, fell off the beak, and floundered apart, sky-walking and laughing.

As I turned to go, she was performing somersaults in the air, in the first blue of that clear morning. And I'd ripped my skirt again.

The ring guided me back to the cave. I didn't have to think about that, so I thought about what Winter had said.

Argul was waiting, sitting against the cave-wall, with a new fire that wasn't visible from outside. I told him what had happened. His face—anger, then laughter. I'll never get used to him. Never want to. Even when we have been years together, I know I will often look at him and start with startled delight.

He said some Raven Guards had gone by, still searching for us, but not very thoroughly. Hadn't even bothered to come near the cave.

I took the diaries out then, from the sewn-in piece under the marriage dress. I opened the first book with care, as if it was too hot. Sat staring.

"It's true, what she said?" he asked. "She got hold of them?"

"It's true."

My horse with the Hulta, this was what Winter had found, or the necklace had. My horse called Sirree. Later, after I was kidnapped, I mentioned Sirree now and then. Somone—Winter—has changed the spelling of Sirree's name to Siree—one R. Very skillfully, so it really looks as if that is the way I have spelled it. Only I wouldn't have.

Did she really do all that and not read it—even the parts about Venn? About Venn and me?

I'll never know.

I'm rather jealous anyway. How unreasonable. Can't help it. But I've thought, Venn only really got interested in me for the most obvious reason. I was the first and only woman he'd seen apart from his mother, and Treacle—who was such a wild thing anyway. So, he sort of fell for me. And I felt keen on him—because he was so like Argul.

But when Venn sees *her*—Winter—*if* she goes there—well. She's stunning. He won't stand a chance. Oh, Venn.

I hope Winter isn't going to turn out like Twilight. Maybe if Winter can only get a life of her own—she won't.

Argul said, "Your hands are like ice."

And right then, as he was warming my hands, this little white thing blew in over the ledge of the cave.

"What's *that?*"

We bent toward it. A small snow-object—no, it was a weeny little *snake*. It gazed up with gentle eyes. And shook its silvery hair.

"Yinyay . . . How—"

"I was called," said Yinyay, her voice rather larger than her size, "by the ring."

"But Venn got you to wipe out all knowledge of Ustareth—"

"The ring," she said, "is still the ring."

"But you're so—little—all this way—from the forest where the Star came down—"

"That pesented no difficulty," she said, "once I had learned enough." And then she grew bigger, in a lovely rippling surge, and stood there on her tail, gazing at us kindly, exactly as I remembered.

"So—the Star-ship's repaired?"

"The ship no longer works," said Yinyay. "But that is unimportant. Since the ring has now connected to me, I am not as I was."

"How *are* you?"

"Now," said Yinyay, "I am the ship."

And she showed us.

Argul and I stood there. For the first time ever, I saw his mouth drop open, as mine is always doing.

For Yinyay, gliding from the cave, balanced there in the blue void between the mountains, began again to grow. And— G—R—O—W—

Up and up went Yinyay. As this happened, her snakelike body straightened out. The white crags reflected on her own polished whiteness. She was tall, and wide. The height of several mansions piled one on another (as they say). Broad as any palace. Straight as a pale sword, but with her excellent metallic face and flowing tinsel hair still there, at the very top.

"That," said Argul, "is a Tower."

It was true. She was. A *Tower*—in the air.

Her mild voice came to us, only humanly loud, but carrying, and melodious as a song.

"I am quite ready now, to receive you, and take you where you wish. Or I can become small again. As small as you find useful. Small enough to fit in a pocket."

For now, we've kept Yinyay as a Tower. She's magnificent. She has magnets, naturally, to deal with gravity. She has seven stories, lifts, windows that clear or close over, machines that make food and drink. Bathrooms. Furniture. A library—! Plants . . . All sorts of things. Everything. As she flew us away, whirling in a protective globe of force, visible—but entirely beyond any attack—we explored our new domain.

Below, the glaciers of the Northern mountains melted away.

I suppose we really are safe now. As safe as you can be, if you're alive in this world.

We've talked about what we may do. Of course there are the Hulta to consider, though Argul has said to me, "I can't really go back, Cluidi. It's Hulta law. Once a leader lets go the leadership, that's it." "*Law!*" I shouted. But he only shook his head. I don't know how this will work out, then.

He did it for me, left them. And Blurn would be a great leader, no matter what Blurn said; otherwise, as Argul told me, the choice would have been impossible.

But he gave up his title, his people, his power—for me.

As Yinyay flies now, this circling Tower, the night has come. We're on the third floor. Soft lamplight and armchairs. Argul is sitting reading a book from Yinyay's library. It's in a language I certainly don't know, all marks like arrows, and squares—

Argul seems at home. None of this, after the first seconds, has thrown him. But he's seen more of the world than I. And well, he's Argul.

I've been writing this up.

What do you think?

Is it going to be all right?

There is a chance the Hulta might, somehow, join us, or we join them, or . . .

But this—is a Tower.

I looked up then and said that to him, to Argul.

He said, "Ustareth" (he never now calls her Zeera) "made this setup. Your Yinyay blossoming into *this*, when the ring started to work again. Ustareth still *thought* in Towers."

"Then this *is* a Tower."

"The other Towers have animal emblems," he said, "Wolves, Ravens—but the top of this Tower has a human face."

A human face. A Human Tower?

We'll marry in Peshamba. Under the CLOCK. They do

weddings there. Neither of us will have a single friend to celebrate with us, not a single family member. His mother and father are dead. Mine are—unknown forever.

Perhaps, though, there is now some way I could rescue some of the girls I knew from the House—Daisy and Pattoo—Dengwi—and Blurn *might* just come to the wedding. And Dagger. I might even get to see Sirree, with two R's, again.

I'll stop writing now. There are so many blank pages left at the end of this book. It worries me a little. Will I still write to you, my friend I'll never meet, in the future? Or will I ever know you, or your name—your names?

Maybe not. But you know *me*, better than most.

What do you say—was Twilight right? Am I this dire thing, the "Wolf Queen?" No, you know I'm not. It's what Argul said: Claidi—a Sheep in Wolf's Clothing.

That's me.